GENERAL QUIZ

Born in an erstwhile landowning family in what was then East Bengal, G. Basu (b. 1943) has had both the inclination and the means to read widely across disciplines. Although not exactly a polymath, his interests range from the liberal arts and the social sciences to applied sciences like technology and medicine. Keenly interested in sports (although no sportsman himself, a typical bhadralok), Basu is a fanatical supporter of East Bengal Club.

GENERAL QUIZ

G. Basu

RUPA

Published by
Rupa Publications India Pvt. Ltd. 2004
7/16, Ansari Road, Daryaganj
New Delhi 110002

Sales centres:
Allahabad Bengaluru Chennai
Hyderabad Jaipur Kathmandu
Kolkata Mumbai

ISBN: 978-81-716-7037-6

Seventh impression 2016

10 9 8 7

The moral right of the author has been asserted.

For Menaka
nevertheless

ACKNOWLEDGEMENT

The author wishes to acknowledge his indebtedness to Mr. R.K. Mehra for providing him with a considerable amount of source material, as also for making concessions for his dilatoriness.

GB

CONTENTS

Quiz 1

1. Under Gorbachev the USSR has launched a number of reformist programmes, one of which is *perestroika*. What exactly is it?
   (a) Relaxation of Communist Party control
   (b) Tolerance of criticism of government policies
   (c) Admission of foreign cultural influences
   (d) Reconstructing the country's social and economic system

2. The Warsaw Treaty Organization (1955) was an answer to the North Atlantic Treaty Organization, or NATO, as it is popularly known. Its members were Albania, Bulgaria, Czechoslovakia, East Germany, Hungary, Poland, Romania, and the Soviet Union. After the Russian suppression of the people's movement, one of the members withdrew. Which?
   (a) Albania (b) Bulgaria (c) Hungary (d) Poland

3. Computer language has developed over the decades, using different acronyms for different functions Which, among the following, predates the others?
   (a) FORTRAN (b) ALGOL (c) BASIC (d) SNOBOL

4. What is the superiority of Arabic numerals over Roman numerals?
   (a) Roman numerals cannot be decimalized (b) Arabic numerals are easier to read (c) Arabic numerals in a series proceed on simple multiplication (d) Arabic numerals have the zero

5. Lawrence Durrell wrote a novel called *Justine*. Who had written a book with the same name much earlier?
   (a) Benjamin Disraeli (b) Henry Fielding (c) Marquis de Sade (d) Emile Zola

6. *Stupas*, large hemispherical domes, containing relics of the Buddha, were raised all over India and some

places abroad. Which among the following places has the earliest *stupa*?

(a) Amaravati (b) Sarnath (c) Bharhut (d) Sanchi

7. Cleopatra, queen of Egypt, was much married and knew many men. Among the following who was her last husband?

(a) Ptolemy XIII (b) Marc Antony (c) Octavius Caesar (d) Ptolemy XIV

8. Of the following countries which one shows a decline, i.e., a negative growth rate, in population?

(a) China (b) Denmark (c) Japan (d) U.K.

9. The internationally accepted borderline between India and China on India's north-east is called the

(a) Durand Line (b) MacMahon Line (c) 38th Parallel (d) The Peking Divide

10. Who was the founder of the doctrine of *advaita* or monism ('there is no second')?

(a) Sankara (b) Ramanuja (c) Madva (d) Abhinava Gupta

11. What is rubella?

(a) Whooping cough (b) German measles (c) Skin eruptions (d) Bleeding of the nose

12. The infection of AIDS occurs through the contamination of

(a) semen (b) mouth (c) blood (d) fingers

13. The following composers have all composed in the twentieth century, early or late. Arrange their names chronologically.

(a) Igor Stravinsky (b) Jean Sibelius (c) Arnold Schoenberg (d) Gustav Mahler

14. Exposure to nuclear radiation is most likely to affect this part of the human body first:

(a) Eyes (b) Blood (c) Bone marrow (d) Kidney

15. Polyantha, Floribunda, Hybrid Tea, Ramblers — what are these types of?

(a) Jasmine (b) Rose (c) Apple (d) Pear

16. Which reference work rates as the all-time best-seller?
    (a) The Concise Oxford Dictionary (b) The Oxford Advanced Learner's Dictionary (c) The Guinness Book of Records (d) Bartholomew's School Atlas
17. What was the ancient name of the Punjab river Jhelum?
    (a) Bipasa (b) Iravati (c) Vitasta (d) Satadru
18. Many of the larger rivers of India originate in or terminate at another neighbouring country. Which is the largest among the completely indigenous rivers?
    (a) Jamur.a (b) Brahmaputra (c) Krishna (d) Godavari
19. It has been repeatedly pointed out by economists who recommend the abolition of income-tax in India and its substitution by an expenditure tax that direct taxes bring in little enough revenue, although their cost of administration is enormous. What percentage of the total Indian tax revenue is brought in by direct taxes?
    (a) 9% (b) 12% (c) 14% (d) 17%
20. What does ambivalent mean?
    (a) Undecided (b) Without the force of conviction (c) Doubting (d) Simultaneous existence of two conflicting attitudes

Quiz 2

21. The Berlin Wall has fallen, and pieces of it are now sold as souvenirs. When was it built?
    (a) 1951 (b) 1956 (c) 1957 (d) 1961
22. Who was the founder of the chemical industry in India?
    (a) The Maharaja of Dhrangadhra (b) Lord Ripon (c) P.C. Ray (d) A. Latif

3

23. A dodecagon is a polygon with
    (a) seven sides (b) nine sides (c) ten sides (d) twelve sides

24. Who invented the jet engine?
    (a) Frank Whittle (b) Heinrich Geissler (c) Charles Babbage (d) Hans Fischer

25. What is the nationality of the Nobel Prize winning novelist Miguel Angel Asturias who wrote *The Green Pope* and *The Eyes of the Interred*?
    (a) Chilean (b) Guatemalan (c) Spanish (d) Mexican

26. When did the Harappan Culture flourish in India?
    (a) *c.* 2500-1500 B.C. (b) *c.* 2000-1200 B.C. (c) *c.* 1500 B.C.-A.D. 500 (d) *c.* 1500-500 B.C.

27. What was the name of Napoleon Bonaparte's first wife?
    (a) Josephine (b) Maria Theresa (c) Marie Louise (d) Eugene

28. Which country in the world produces all the following precious metals in substantial quantities: gold, silver, platinum, diamonds, industrial diamonds?
    (a) Colombia (b) South Africa (c) USSR (d) Canada

29. Where is America's Statue of Liberty located?
    (a) Staten Island (b) Liberty Island (c) Fifth Avenue (d) Ellis Island

30. The chant of *Gayatri* is considered the most holy passage of the most holy text, *Rig Veda*. To which god is it addressed?
    (a) Brahma (b) Vishnu (c) Surya (d) Shiva

31. What exactly is thrombosis, from variants of which people die?
    (a) Sudden stoppage of the heart (b) Sudden death of the brain, leading to a collapse of the heart (c) Obstruction of the artery or vein by a clot of blood (d) Obstruction of artery only by a clot of blood

32. Which of the following vitamins are water soluble, and are quickly expelled through urine, thus rarely causing toxic reaction?
(a) A (b) B Complex (c) C (d) E

33. Ananda K. Coomaraswamy (1877-1947), art historian, was one of the most eminent interpreters of Indian art. What was his nationality?
(a) Indian (b) British (c) Ceylonese (d) American

34. Painters like Matisse, Vlaminick, Braque, and Dufy were called Fauvists. What does *fauve* mean?
(a) Loud colours (b) Wild beast (c) Immoralist (d) Distortionist

35. How would you distinguish between an Indian elephant and an African elephant?
(a) The African elephant will have long curved tusks
(b) The African elephant will have a very long tail
(c) The African elephant will have small feet (d) The African elephant will have larger ears

36. *Metamorphosis* is the story of a man who wakes up one morning to find that he has been transformed into a giant insect. Who is the author of this modern classic?
(a) Franz Kafka (b) Stefan Zweig (c) Vladimir Nabokov (d) Günter Grass

37. The five rivers of Punjab, the derivation of the State's name, are:
(a) Sutlej, Ravi, Beas, Chenab, and Jhelum
(b) Yamuna, Saraswati, Ravi, Beas, and Jhelum
(c) Ravi, Beas, Jhelum, Indus, and Yamuna (d) Indus, Ravi, Beas, Jhelum, and Yamuna

38. On the basis of a minute prepared by the Law Member of the Governor-General's Council, on 7 March 1835 the Council decided that henceforth all the public funds would be spent on English education, thus sealing the fate of liberal education in the local languages. Who wrote the minute?

(a) William Adam (b) Sir Charles Wood (c) T.B. Macaulay (d) The first Lord Hardinge

39. No sensible person should proclaim, 'My country right or wrong', for it is like saying ,'My mother drunk or sober'. Who gave this sane advice?
(a) George Bernard Shaw (b) Oscar Wilde (c) G.K. Chesterton (d) A.J.P. Taylor

40. Choose the precise meaning of kitsch.
(a) Trendy art or literature (b) Action painting (c) Commercialized human relations (d) Vulgarized art

Quiz 3

41. What is *samizdat* literature?
(a) Literature imbued with the ideals of the Soviet Socialist Republics (b) Clandestine printing and distribution of dissident literature in the USSR (c) The literature of the new Left (d) Literature stressing the individual, rather than the collective, values

42. Light travels at the rate of 300,000 km per second. What distance will it travel in one light year?
(a) 115 million km (b) 450 million km (c) 495 million km (d) 9.5 million million km

43. Gunmetal was originally used for making guns, although now its main use is in casting machine parts. What go to make this alloy?
(a) Iron, brass, and tin (b) Copper, tin, and zinc (c) Iron, tin, and feldspar (d) Titanium, iron, and zinc

44. Synthetic vinegar is nothing but this acid, diluted:
(a) Acetic acid (b) Hydrochloric acid (c) Ascorbic acid (d) Citric acid

45. The nursery rhyme goes, 'Here we go round the –. bush ... on a cold and frosty morning.' Which bush?

(a) Hawthorn (b) Gooseberry (c) Mulberry
(d) Cranberry
46. When in 1975 Sikkim became an Indian State what
was its position in the order of States?
(a) 20th (b) 21st (c) 22nd (d) 23rd
47. Constantinople, once the capital of the Byzantine
empire, and known as Byzantium, was the most
splendid of European cities, famed for its architecture and literary and artistic treasures. It fell to the
Turks and the contents of its libraries got dispersed
in Europe. When did Constantinople fall?
(a) A.D. 1256 (b) 1261 (c) 1453 (d) 1496
48. The river Liffey flows through a capital city. Identify
which.
(a) Bucharest (b) Paris (c) Dublin (d) Athens
49. Which countries does the 49th parallel divide?
(a) France and Germany (b) Finland and Russia
(c) The United States and Canada (d) South Africa
and Namibia
50. We are living in the darkest of ages, *kali*. It is
important to know (is it really?) how long the
kaliyuga is supposed to last. Guess.
(a) 8,000 years (b) 80,000 years (c) 167,500 years
(d) 432,000 years
51. Podiatry is a science of the diseases of the
(a) mouth (b) rectum (c) teeth (d) feet
52. Which of the following is the longest-living creature
on earth?
(a) Tortoise (b) Elephant (c) Gorilla (d) Man
53. Mendelssohn was a famous nineteenth century
German composer, one of whose major composi-
tions was the Overture to *A Midsummer Night's
Dream*. What was his full name?
(a) Moses Mendelssohn (b) Gregor Johann Mendelssohn (c) Karl Augustus Mendelssohn (d) Felix
Mendelssohn

54. Art Deco is a style of interior decoration, jewellery, architecture, etc., at its height in the 1930s, enjoying a revival in the 1970s and 1980s. What is its characteristic?

(a) Heavy, weighty ornamentation (b) Detailed filigree work (c) Asymmetric designs aimed at arresting the viewer's attention (d) Geometrical, symmetrical, utilitarian designs adapted to mass production

55. Electric fish, like the eel, the catfish, and the ray can generate powerful electric charges to deter enemies and paralyse prey. How strong can the charge be?

(a) 200 volts (b) 260 volts (c) 500 volts (d) 600 volts

56. Many people have grown up with Penguin Books. When was the first batch published?

(a) 1928 (b) 1932 (c) 1935 (d) 1937

57. Oriental dramas precede other dramas, and among oriental dramas, Sanskrit dramas, which flourished from 1500 B.C., are the oldest. Which among the following was the earliest known playwright?

(a) Bhavabhuti (b) Kalidasa (c) Bana (d) Bhasa

58. The value of the rupee, i.e., its purchasing power, is steadily declining over the years, so that fairly high salaries, say Rs. 6000 per month in 1990, doesn't mean much at all. What would have been its equivalent in 1960-61?

(a) Rs. 600 (b) Rs. 780 (c) Rs. 840 (d) Rs. 960

59. What is a hamster?

(a) It is a North American singing bird (b) It is a small fish found in Arctic waters (c) It is a bad actor who thinks that mouthing out the lines of a dialogue is the best way to create a dramatic effect (d) It is a rodent, a serious agricultural pest

60. Christian Dior, Papa Meilland, Queen Elizabeth, Oklahoma — what are these names of?

(a) Perfume (b) Bone China (c) Roses (d) Apples

Quiz 4

61. The North Atlantic Treaty Organization, or NATO, is a military alliance between certain member nations. Of the following, one is not a NATO member. Who?
    (a) Iceland (b) Belgium (c) Portugal (d) Spain
62. Earth's atmosphere, which extends up to 80 km above, has the following gaseous constituents in the main. Arrange them in a descending order of percentage.
    (a) Carbon dioxide (b) Oxygen (c) Nitrogen (d) Argon
63. Several novels about the Sepoy Mutiny have been written by Indians as well as Englishmen. Who wrote *The Siege of Krishnapur?*
    (a) J.G. Farrell (b) M.M. Kaye (c) John Masters (d) Paul Scott
64. Of the following martial arts, two are related. Which two?
    (a) Karate (b) Judo (c) Kendo (d) Jujitsu
65. Who defeated Muhammad Ali in 1978 in the World Heavyweight Championship?
    (a) Larry Holmes (b) Leon Spink (c) Teofilo Stevenson (d) Mike Tyson
66. The Meiji Restoration in Japan (1868), which overthrew the Tokugawa Shogunate, a military dictatorship which ruled Japan, had certain important outcomes. Which was the most important?
    (a) It established constitutional monarchy (b) It brought about the downfall of feudalism (c) It used Western armaments for the first time to expel the foreigners (d) It reformed the army along modern lines
67. Where is the world's largest gas field located?
    (a) Saudi Arabia (b) USSR (c) Iraq (d) Nigeria

9

68. After blood circulation stops, how long does the brain take to die?
(a) It dies immediately (b) 90 seconds (c) Three minutes (d) Between four and five minutes

69. When did Indian materialism, known under various labels like Charvakadarshan, Lokayata, and Ajivika, first flourish?
(a) c. 600 B.C. (b) A.D. 200-300 (c) Around A.D. 900 (d) A.D. 530

70. The fifth Sikh Guru compiled the First Sacred Book, *Adi Granth*, by collecting verses mainly from his four predecessors, as well as those from some Hindu and Muslim saints. What is the name of this Guru?
(a) Guru Angad (b) Guru Amardas (c) Guru Arjan (d) Guru Ramdas

71. For which vitamin is human requirement assumed, but not proved?
(a) B_2 (b) E (c) K (d) Biotin

72. Which disease is gingivitis?
(a) Disturbed hearing (b) Itching of feet (c) Inflammation of gums (d) Periodic bleeding from the nose

73. Who composed Piano Sonata No. 14, also known as the *Moonlight Sonata*?
(a) Mozart (b) Chopin (c) Handel (d) Mendelssohn

74. Like a man in relation to his environment, a tree in relation to its environment is the subject of a special branch of science. What is it called?
(a) Sylvan ecology (b) Systems ecology (c) Forest autecology (d) Synecology

75. In Conan Doyle's *Hound of the Baskervilles*, Sir Henry hears a howling on the moor and tells Watson that it is the noise made by a hound, for he knows their call. Which of the following species would qualify?
(a) Alsatian (b) Great Dane (c) Dalmatian (d)Beagle

76. Perhaps the most comic novel on war written in English is *Catch-22*. Who wrote it?

(a) Norman Mailer (b) Irwin Shaw (c) Robert Graves (d) Joseph Heller

77. India's population is growing at an alarming rate, in spite of *nasbandi* and other high-minded efforts. We have the record of growth in the ten years between 1971 and 1981. What was it?
(a) 15% (b) 20% (c) 23% (d) 25%

78. Just as the Indian government has set a target for Education for All, 1995, it has Health for All in mind by a certain year. What is the target date?
(a) 2000 (b) 2001 (c) 2005 (d) 2007

79. Which is the world's oldest free public city library supported by municipal taxes?
(a) Bibliotheque nationale, Paris (b) The British Museum (c) New York Public Library (d) Boston Public Library

80. What is the meaning of juxtaposition?
(a) Contrasting two opposite things (b) Laying side by side (c) Violent conflict (d) Comparing two possible solutions

Quiz 5

81. The domino theory holds that if one country becomes Communist, other countries in that region will follow, like falling dominoes in a line. Who first applied the theory to describe a contemporary political phenomenon?
(a) President Eisenhower (b) President Kennedy (c) Henry Kissinger (d) Robert McNamara

82. Cabal now means a small group of political intriguers. Originally, the word was an acronym of the names of five ministers who helped a king rule: Clifford, Ashley, Buckingham, Arlington, and Lauderdale. Who was the king?
(a) Charles I (b) Charles II (c) James II (d) George III

83. During the Cultural Revolution Mao decreed nine categories of enemies, and these included landlords, rich peasants, counter-revolutionaries, rightists, etc. The ninth category he called the stinking ninth. Who could they be?

(a) Moneylenders (b) Industrialists (c) Capitalist-roaders (d) Intellectuals

84. The flight recorder, salvaged from the wreckage of an aircrash to provide clues to the mishap, is a strong box with a distinctive colour, which is

(a) yellow (b) orange (c) black (d) bright green

85. Who was the recipient of the first Bharatiya Jnanpith award?

(a) Mahadevi Verma (Hindi) (b) Umashankar Joshi (Gujarati) (c) Ka Naa Subramanyam (Tamil) (d) G. Shankara Kurup (Malayalam)

86. In Judo parlance what is a *shiaijo*?

(a) The referee (b) The contestants (c) The fighting area (d) The Black Belt

87. The weapon in the Japanese martial art kendo has changed. What is it now?

(a) Pointed sticks (b) Bamboo poles (c) Bamboo swords (d) Baton

88. During World War II the Afrika Corps led by General Rommel routed the British. In the British counter-attack, however, the German army was decimated. Who led the British attack?

(a) General Montgomery (b) General Wavell (c) General Alexander (d) Field Marshal Auchinlek

89. Where in the world are the great vampire bats found?

(a) North Africa (b) Sri Lanka (c) Mexico (d) Paraguay

90. In which country is Marienbad, an internationally famous health resort, located?

(a) Germany (b) Austria (c) Switzerland (d) Czechoslovakia

91. What is the Golden Rule?

    (a) Regret not the past (b) Do not a borrower or a lender be (c) Do unto others as you would have them do unto you (d) Follow the Golden Mean — the moderate path

92. Although the Digambara sect of Jains hold that Mahavira never married, others record the name of his wife and daughter. What was the wife's name?

    (a) Trishala (b) Yashodhara (c) Yashoda (d) Priyadarshana

93. Socially unacceptable diseases are often called by another, deceptive name. What is Hansen's disease really?

    (a) Syphilis (b) Leprosy (c) AIDS (d) Impotence

94. Ananda K. Coomaraswamy, born in Ceylon, was a famous art critic, who has done important work on India's art and culture. What does his middle name stand for?

    (a) Kentish (b) Kuruvilla (c) Krishnaswamy (d) Krishna

95. Hippopotamus, the male of which species weighs about five tons, is related to a quite well-known animal, as cats are to tigers. Which animal?

    (a) Elephant (b) Horse (c) Rhinoceros (d) Pig

96. 'The Short Happy Life of Francis Macomber' and 'The Killers' are two of the most memorable short stories in English written in the present century. Can you name the author?

    (a) William Faulkner (b) Ernest Hemingway (c) Saul Bellow (d) W. Somerset Maugham

97. Who was the first Indian High Commissioner in Britain?

    (a) V.K.R.V. Rao (b) C.D. Deshmukh (c) Sir Saros Jehangir Cowasjee (d) V.K. Krishna Menon

98. Whose unremitting labour and strenuous agitation led to the passing of the Hindu Widows Remarriage

Act, 1856? (He even gave his own son in marriage with a widow)

(a) Raja Rammohun Roy (b) Mr. Justice Mahadev Govinda Ranade (c) Gopal Krishna Gokhale (d) Ishwar Chandra Vidyasagar

99. For how many weeks did *Mahabharat* run on the Doordarshan?

(a) 80 weeks (b) 90 weeks (c) 93 weeks (d) 97 weeks

100. What does inane mean?

(a) Stupid (b) Wrong headed (c) Senseless and unimaginative (d) Perverse

Quiz 6

101. Which of the following groups of countries founded the non-aligned movement?

(a) India, Sri Lanka, Japan (b) India, Bangladesh, Egypt (c) India, Yugoslavia, Egypt (d) India, Japan, Switzerland

102. In our solar system which planet takes the longest time to orbit the sun?

(a) Jupiter (b) Pluto (c) Mars (d) Saturn

103. Just as in Marlowe's *Dr. Faustus* there is a memorable description of Helen of Troy, in Shakespeare's *Antony and Cleopatra* there are some beautiful lines on Cleopatra:

> 'Age cannot wither her, nor custom stale
> Her infinite variety. Other women cloy
> The appetites they feed, but she makes hungry
> Where most she satisfies ...'

— Who pays this tribute?

(a) Octavius (b) Enobarbus (c) Pompey (c) Ventidius

104. When did India last win the Olympic gold in hockey?

(a) 1976 (b) 1980 (c) 1984 (d) 1964

105. What is the duration of a normal hockey match?
(a) 60 minutes (b) 70 minutes (c) 75 minutes (d) 90 minutes

106. What is Charlotte Corday remembered as?
(a) Napoleon's mistress (b) An eighteenth century opera singer of distinction (c) As the assassin of Jean Paul Marat (d) A great actress of neo-classical drama

107. Which is the world's longest canal system?
(a) Suez Canal (b) Volga-Baltic Canal System (c) St. Lawrence Seaway (d) Kiel Canal

108. The Republic of Ivory Coast is one of the largest producers in the world of
(a) cocoa (b) elephant tusks (c) mahogany (d) oil

109. He is the sixth incarnation of Vishnu, born as the son of the sage Yamadagni. Once the Kshatriya king Kartavirya despoiled his father's ashrama and killed him. In revenge he rid the earth of Kshatriyas as many as seventeen times. Who was this incarnation?
(a) Rama (b) Balarama (c) Parasurama (d) Kalki

110. A moral and religious system of ethical precepts for the management of society, based on the practice of *jen* — sympathy or human-heartedness — as shown in one's relations with others and demonstrated through adherence to *li*, a combination of ethic and ritual — what is it called?
(a) Confucianism (b) Taoism (c) Buddhism (d) Zen Buddhism

111. In good maternity hospitals a vaccine is compulsorily administered some weeks before delivery. Which is it?
(a) BCG (b) Tetanus (c) Salk vaccine (d) Sabin vaccine

112. Rainer Warner Fassbinder, 1946-82, was a renowned German film-maker. Can you identify his film among the following?
(a) *Lift to the Scaffold* (b) *The Moment of Truth* (c) *David Holzman's Diary* (d) *The Marriage of Maria Braun*

113. The Forest (Conservation) Act was the outcome of the increasing ecological concern of the country. It prohibits the diversion of forest land to non-forest use. When was the Act passed?
(a) 1951 (b) 1967 (c) 1978 (d) 1980
114. The Piranha is a freshwater fish which often kills cattle and men with its strong jaws and sharp cutting teeth. In which river are they mostly found?
(a) Zambezi (b) Amazon (c) Congo (d) Hwang Ho
115. Perry Mason, the detective, is the creation of
(a) John Dickson Carr (b) Michael Innes (c) Ellery Queen (d) Erle Stanley Gardner
116. Equal work, equal pay, i.e., for both the sexes, was guaranteed by the Equal Remuneration Act quite late in India. How late?
(a) 1974 (b) 1976 (c) 1978 (d) 1980
117. Who took the initiative in founding the Indian National Congress in 1885?
(a) David Octavian Hume (b) W.C. Bonnerjea (c) Surendra Nath Banerjea (d) Mrs. Annie Besant
118. Mata Hari was accused of espionage, tried by the French and executed. What was her nationality?
(a) German; Mata Hari was a stage name (b) Japanese (c) French (d) Dutch
119. In advertising what is knocking copy?
(a) Advertising text that completely convinces a prospective buyer (b) Advertising matter that is repeated over a long period (c) Advertising material which names and criticises a rival's product (d) Weak-kneed, unconvincing advertising text
120. What does perspicacious mean?
(a) Sweating (b) One who can see a very long distance (c) Honest and open (d) Acutely perceptive

121. The Geheimes Staatspolizei or the Gestapo was one of the most feared organs of the Nazi State. What was its function?
(a) Extermination of the Jews (b) Arrest of Jews, Communists, and Catholics (c) Policing the newly occupied territories of Nazi Germany (d) Working as the secret police

122. Vesicants, lachrymators, sternutators — these are only some members of their class, which is what?
(a) Food preserving agents (b) Balms of different kinds (c) Industrial gases (d) Poison gases

123. Jacob Grimm, together with his brother Wilhelm Grimm, wrote a number of fairy tales which are still widely read. Jacob, however, was quite famous in another field. Which?
(a) Medicine (b) Law (c) Philology (d) Economics

124. Which Indian is reckoned to have scored more than a thousand goals in international hockey?
(a) Ajit Pal Singh (b) Roop Singh (c) Dhyan Chand (d) Jaipal Singh

125. In which year did Prakash Padukone win the All-England Badminton title?
(a) 1976 (b) 1978 (c) 1980 (d) 1982

126. The first batch of 102 English Puritans arrived on the east coast of America in 1602. What was the name of the ship they sailed in?
(a) *The Voyager* (b) *Westward Ho* (c) *Mayflower* (d) *Discoverer*

127. In which country lies the source of the river Nile?
(a) Egypt (b) Sudan (c) Zaire (d) Uganda

128. Among the African cities, whose population is the highest?
(a) Johannesburg (b) Lagos (c) Cairo (d) Kinshasa

129. The reformist Hindu sect known as the Brahmo Samaj, originally Brahmo Sabha, was founded in 1828. Who was its founder?
(a) Debendranath Tagore (b) Keshub Chandra Sen (c) Raja Rammohun Roy (d) Akshay Kumar Datta

130. After receiving enlightenment, where did Buddha preach his first sermon?
(a) Rajagriha (b) Sravasti (c) Vaishali (d) Rishipattan

131. Antibiotics may have harmful side effects. What is the possible side effect of Streptomycin?
(a) Diarrhoea (b) Involuntary emission (c) Deafness (d) Visual blackouts

132. *La Giaconda* is one of the world's most famous paintings. What is its popular name?
(a) *Adoration of the Magi* (b) *Madonna of the Rocks* (c) *Olympia* (d) *Mona Lisa*

133. In which State is the Periyar Game Sanctuary located?
(a) Karnataka (b) Tamil Nadu (c) Kerala (d) Gujarat

134. Where did the recently extinct bird Dodo live?
(a) Egypt (b) South Africa (c) Mauritius (d) Solomon Islands

135. Copyright is the author's exclusive right of control of an original work of writing. How long does it last?
(a) 50 years from his death (b) 50 years since its date of publication (c) A period of 75 years after the death of the author (d) 50 years after the death of the author or the date of publication, whichever is later

136. This name is so often misspelt that it deserves a quiz. Identify the correct spelling.
(a) Ram Mohan Roy (b) Rammohun Roy (c) Ram Mohun Roy (d) Ram Mohan Ray

137. When was the Gold Control Ordinance, later to become an Act, first promulgated fixing the maxi-

mum purity of gold, which could be sold (not old gold recycled into new ornaments) at 14 carats?
(a) 1963 (b) 1965 (c) 1966 (d) 1967

138. In the U.S. education system there is an institution called normal school. What is it?
(a) Racially unsegregated school (b) Socially mixed school, i.e., enrolling children of all economic strata (c) Elementary teachers' training school (d) Vocational studies school

139. The IQ of a genius is above 140. What should be the IQ of a normally intelligent person?
(a) Around 100 (b) 115 (c) 80 (d) 75

140. What is the meaning of obstreperous?
(a) Noisy and rough (b) Obstructive (c) High-spirited (d) Obstinate

Quiz 8

141. What does apartheid literally mean?
(a) Racial segregation (b) Separate development (c) Remaining apart (d) Purity of blood

142. In our solar system which planet takes the least time to orbit the sun?
(a) Venus (b) Mercury (c) Earth (d) Mars

143. When was the first complete collection of Shakespeare's plays, known as the First Folio, published? Shakespeare's dates are 1564-1616.
(a) 1623 (b) 1618 (c) 1627 (d) 1615

144. Who is the youngest heavyweight boxing champion of the world?
(a) Mike Tyson (b) Cassius Clay (c) Joe Louis (d) Leon Spink

145. Where did figure-skating originate?
(a) Sweden (b) France (c) England (d) Iceland

146. Which king's or queen's reign has been the longest in English history?

(a) Queen Elizabeth (b) George III (c) Queen Victoria (d) Queen Elizabeth II

147. Which is the world's largest sweet-water lake?
    (a) Lake Superior (b) Lake Victoria (c) Baikal (d) Lake Michigan

148. The world's longest river systems are the Nile (4160 miles), the Amazon (3900 miles), the Missouri (3740 miles), and the Ob (3460 miles). Which country could the Ob flow through?
    (a) Nigeria (b) Russia (c) China (d) Canada

149. Which country has volcanoes that spew not fire and brimstone, but mud?
    (a) Sri Lanka (b) Brunei (c) New Zealand (d) Philippines

150. King Pyrrhus of Epirus went to Italy in 280 B.C. and defeated the Romans. This was the Pyrrhic victory. What does it exactly mean?
    (a) Victory against overwhelmingly stronger forces
    (b) Victory against a weak and decadent power
    (c) Victory gained by great bloodshed and large-scale massacre (d) Victory in which the losses almost outweigh the gains

151. In case of poor vision the first test an eye specialist administers is the reading of the Snellen chart. What is the distance from which this chart is meant to be read?
    (a) 4 metres (b) 6 metres (c) 5 metres (d) 10 metres

152. Edith Head, Madeleine Vionnet, Elsa Schiaparelli, and Mary Quant — what do these ladies have in common?
    (a) They are all fashion designers (b) They are all renowned ballerinas (c) Film actresses from the last four decades (d) They are all renowned sopranos

153. Which is the most treeless State in India?
    (a) Bihar (b) Rajasthan (c) Haryana (d) Orissa

154. Which are the largest birds in the world?

(a) The Great Indian Bustard (b) Wild Eagles
(c) Emu (d) Condors

155. In which book of his did Conan Doyle first introduce the fictional detective Sherlock Holmes?
(a) *A Study in Scarlet* (b) *The Adventures of Sherlock Holmes* (c) *The Hound of the Baskervilles* (d) *The Adventure of the Redheaded League*

156. Which Indian State is the best afforested?
(a) Assam (b) Meghalaya (c) Arunachal Pradesh (d) Orissa

157. Which was the first direct translation of a Sanskrit work into English?
(a) *Rig Veda* by Max Mueller (b) *Manu Smriti* by Sir William Jones (c) Charles Wilkins's *Bhagavad Gita* (d) William Jones's *Shakuntala*

158. In countries where public life is corrupt, there is often talk (only talk, mostly) of appointing ombudsmen, officials who would investigate citizens' complaints against the government or its servants. Which language does the word come from?
(a) Dutch (b) German (c) Norwegian (d) Swedish

159. In what sort of punishment was a gibbet (pronounced 'jibbet') used in former times?
(a) Hanging (b) Beheading (c) Drawing and quartering (d) Crucifying

160. What is the meaning of fractious?
(a) Quarrelsome (b) Holding a different opinion (c) Unruly (d) Divisive

Quiz 9

161. Who are the Khmer Rouge?
(a) Cambodian guerrilla Communist force (b) Laotian Communist guerrilla force (c) Vietnamese Communist guerrilla force (d) Thai Communist force

162. Boolean algebra, which is used in computer science. is an algebraic manipulation of logical statements. When did the English mathematician George Boole develop it?

(a) 1827 (b) 1850 (c) 1896 (d) 1907

163. How many sides go to make a trapezium?

(a) 3 (b) 4 (c) 5 (d) 6

164. One of the all-time greats in tennis, she won all eight Wimbledon titles she entered for. Who is she?

(a) Martina Navratilova (b) Billie Jean King (c) Helen Wills Moody (d) Evonne Goolagong

165. In which country was the first World Cup Football Tournament held?

(a) Uruguay (b) Brazil (c) Argentina (d) Belgium

166. Mesopotamia, the ancient region in west Asia, called 'the cradle of civilization', flourished between 5000 B.C. and A.D. 1258. In which State is it now?

(a) Iraq (b) Iran (c) Syria (d) Egypt

167. Which among the following airports is the farthest from London?

(a) Auckland (b) Tokyo (c) Sydney (d) Brisbane

168. Which country in Africa is entirely surrounded by another country?

(a) Swaziland (b) Lesotho (c) Zimbabwe (d) Malawi

169. Buridan's ass typified one particular psychological trait, viz.,

(a) presumption; it thought it could roar like a lion (b) meekness; it stood still while its back was being overloaded, until the back broke (c) indecision; standing in front of two equally good piles of hay it found no reason to choose one over the other, and starved to death (d) resignation; did exactly what asses are supposed to do, viz., did its work and chewed its hay, and thus found utter contentment

170. The chief symptom of Down's syndrome is
(a) A rickety appearance (b) A total absence of retentive memory (c) Stammering (d) Severe mental and physical retardation

171. What is the real name of Bob Dylan?
(a) Lech Kapucinski (b) Arthur Longbottom (c) Robert Zimmerman (d) Jeremy Twit

172. Hydroponics has obviously something to do with water. What exactly?
(a) A science which studies the chemical properties of fluids (b) Study of the distribution and movement of water through land surfaces (c) Underwater reception and interpretation of sound waves (d) Soilless cultivation of plants

173. What disease are you liable to contract if you visit a bat-infested cave?
(a) Diphtheria (b) Rabies (c) Tetanus (d) Asthma

174. Who was the first recipient of the Nobel Prize in Literature in 1901?
(a) George Bernard Shaw (b) H.G. Wells (c) Leo Tolstoy (d) R.F.A. Sully-Prudhomme

175. The Roman Emperor Nero, who is supposed to have fiddled while Rome burnt, and whose last words were, 'What an artist the world is losing in me!', was the first prosecutor of Christians in Rome. The novel *Quo Vadis* was written about Christianity in his time. Who wrote it?
(a) Alexandre Dumas (b) Robert Graves (c) Henrik Sienkiewicz (d) Nathalie Sarraute

176. Who is the founder of the Forward Bloc of India?
(a) Asoka Mehta (b) Asaf Ali (c) J.B. Kripalani (d) Subhas Chandra Bose

177. Next to the Golden Triangle, there is a region called the Golden Crescent, where most of the world's opium -- the raw material of heroin — is grown. Where is the crescent?

(a) The border between Vietnam and China (b) The Burma-Thailand border (c) The Pak-Afghan border (d) The Thailand-Malaysia crescent

178. When a crime or a criminal extends beyond the borders of a country, i.e., when the crime is organized on an international scale, such as in smuggling or the narcotics trade, and when the criminal is known to have crossed the borders of one country, the help of Interpol is sought. What is its full name?

(a) International Police Organization (b) International Police (c) International Criminal Police (d) International Criminal Police Organization

179. What is serendipity?

(a) Sixth sense (b) Knowledge of the future (c) Extreme old age (d) The knack of making fortunate discoveries by accident

180. What is the meaning of bizarre?

(a) Odd or unusual (b) Supernatural (c) Fearsome (d) Gruesome

Quiz 10

181. 'Well, and what was so remarkable about [him]? He executed 460 scholars. We, we executed 46,000 of them; ... You think you insult us by saying we are like [him], but you make a mistake, we have passed him a hundred times.' Unmistakably the defiant boasting of the Cultural Revolution, and its leader, Mao. But who is *him*? The man, incidentally, buried alive 460 scholars who had criticised him.

(a) Kublai Khan (b) Qin Shi Huangdi (c) Chiang Kai-Shek (d) Zhu Ma Hun

182. One of the differences between iron and steel is that steel does not corrode as iron does. Which of the following is mixed with iron to impart corrosion resistance?

(a) Chromium (b) Magnesium (c) Nickel (d) Zinc

183. One of Marilyn Monroe's husbands was the American playwright Arthur Miller, and he wrote a play particularly for her. From the following of his plays which one is it?
(a) *The Death of a Salesman* (b) *The Misfits* (c) *Crucibles* (d) *After the Fall*

184. Which gymnast was the first to achieve the perfect score of 10 in the Olympics?
(a) Vera Caslavska (b) Ludmila Tourischeva (c) Nadia Comaneci (d) Li Ning

185. Which stroke is the slowest in swimming?
(a) Freestyle (b) Backstroke (c) Breaststroke (d) Butterfly

186. The two main branches of Russian socialism before the Revolution were the Bolsheviks and the Mensheviks. As everyone knows, the Bolsheviks were led by Lenin. Who led the Mensheviks?
(a) Kerensky (b) Plekhanov (c) Trotsky (d) Bukharin

187. What are the fastest trains in Germany called?
(a) Intercity (b) Superfast (c) Schnellzug (d) Bullet

188. The Grand Canal is the world's longest (1600 km) man-made canal. Where is it located?
(a) Beijing (b) Venice (c) Amsterdam (d) Copenhagen

189. Which is the largest church of the Christian world?
(a) Saint Peter's Church (b) Saint Paul's Cathedral (c) Saint Mark's Church (d) Saint Patrick's Cathedral

190. Before he became a disciple of Jesus, what was Matthew's occupation?
(a) Farming (b) Fishing (c) Tax collecting (d) Soldiering

191. How can one prevent cataract of the eyes?
(a) By putting regular drops of Cineraria Maritima Succus (b) By regularly putting drops of pure honey

into the eyes (c) By a combination of homoeopathic medicines (d) No way

192. Of the following ballet companies which one is the oldest?

(a) Bolshoi Ballet, Moscow (b) Royal Ballet, London (c) Royal Danish Ballet, Copenhagen (d) Kirov Ballet, Leningrad

193. In Keats's 'Ode to a Nightingale' there is a reference to 'charmed magic casements opening on the foam of perilous seas', which is said to owe its inspiration to a painting by Claude Lorrain. Can you name the painting?

(a) *The Faery Princess* (b) *The Enchanted Castle* (c) *The Forsaken Castle* (d) *The Castle by the Sea*

194. Where is the Valley of Flowers, a riot of colours, located?

(a) California (b) Sicily (c) Garhwal Himalayas (d) Honolulu

195. A day in the year in this city is earmarked for insect trading. Which city is it?

(a) Seoul (b) Beijing (c) Acupulco (d) Frankfurt

196. In which novel does Bernard Malamud describe the career of a baseball player?

(a) *The Natural* (b) *The Assistant* (c) *The Tenant* (d) *A New Life*

197. What is the percentage of the educated unemployed in India in relation to the total number of the unemployed?

(a) 31.5% (b) 37.2% (c) 45.6% (d) 46.8%

198. At what rate is the world population increasing in the 1990-2000 decade?

(a) One new birth every second (b) One new birth every three seconds (c) Two births every second (d) Three births every second

199. Mainstreaming as an educational practice has gained wide acceptance in educational planning since 1960. What is it?

(a) Not providing special learning opportunities to exceptionally bright children, but putting them in the classroom with children of varying attainments (b) Not providing special schools for handicapped children, but putting them in regular classes (c) Selecting the most advanced children and providing them with special guidance to form the main stream of a school's achievement (d) Striving to achieve an average of excellence for all children in a class.

200. What is the meaning of chiaroscuro?
(a) Dusk (b) Early hours of dawn (c) Dark and obscure at the same time (d) An assemblage of bright and dull colours

Quiz 11

201. Who said, 'A revolution is not a dinner party'?
(a) Lenin (b) Marx (c) Mao (d) Ho Chi Minh
202. Archimedes's Principle states that
(a) the weight of water displaced by an immersed body is the same as the body's weight (b) a body immersed in water will sink if it is heavier than the volume of water it displaces (c) a body immersed in water will float if its mass is less than the volume of water it displaces (d) a body immersed in liquid experiences an upward force equal to the weight of the displaced liquid.
203. The French novelist and existentialist philosopher Jean-Paul Sartre refused the Nobel Prize for Literature. Another novelist, however, was forced to refuse it by the Soviet authorities. Who is he?
(a) Joseph Brodsky (b) Alexander Solzhenitsyn (c) M.A. Sholokhov (d) Boris Pasternak
204. Roger Bannister was the first to run the mile under four minutes in 1954. What distinguished position did he hold in later life?

(a) England's sprinting coach (b) President, Board of Trade (c) President of an Oxford college (d) Chairman, Lloyds Bank

205. When did the Asian Games start?
(a) 1948 (b) 1951 (c) 1953 (d) 1954

206. Of the following consorts of King Henry VIII of England who survived the king?
(a) Catherine Howard (b) Catherine Parr (c) Anne Boleyn (d) Jane Seymour

207. How many States does the USA comprise?
(a) 48 (b) 49 (c) 50 (d) 51

208. The Mafia is a secret society which commits organized crime, mostly extraction. Where does it have its origin?
(a) Catalonia (b) Naples (c) Chicago (d) Sicily

209. King Pandu was stricken with the curse that if he ever slept with either of his wives, Kunti or Madri, he would die. Pandu therefore advised Kunti to get a child through someone else, and Kunti followed the advice. Who became Yudhisthira's father?
(a) Surya (b) Narada (c) Indra (d) Yama

210. What is the rate of growth of hair on a normal human head?
(a) 1″ in 4-6 weeks (b) 3″ every month (c) 6″ every month (d) 1.5″ every two weeks

211. This famous bird sanctuary was at one time the most dangerous place for birds to be in, for the local rajah would invite the white rulers for a shoot, and in a single day as many as 4000 birds could be killed. Which is it?
(a) Nalsarovar in Gujarat (b) Manas in Assam (c) Bharatpur in Rajasthan (d) Similipal in Orissa

212. One more or less knows what bacteriological warfare means, employment of deadly bacteria to decimate a population, delivered through warheads or aerosol packages. What then is biological warfare?

(a) The same as bacteriological warfare (b) The use of long-range harmful rays to interfere with the enemies' physical system (c) The use of human beings and animals to fight battles, somewhat like the good old days of World War I (d) Offensive mounted against a country or a race of people on the supposed biological theory that certain people are inherently depraved and ought to be liquidated.

213. Which endearing character in children's fiction was a student of St Custard's?
(a) Smike in *Nicholas Nickleby* (b) Tom Brown in *Tom Brown's School Days* (c) Nigel Molesworth in *Down with Skool* (d) Bertie Wooster in *Thank You, Jeeves*

214. Arrange the following Russian authors chronologically.
(a) Dostoevsky (b) Gogol (c) Pushkin (d) Tolstoy

215. The National Film Archive, founded in 1964, has a collection of nearly 7000 films from all over the world. Where is it located?
(a) Bombay (b) Pune (c) Delhi (d) Calcutta

216. 'Petit bourgeois mentality' is a term of abuse. Who really are the petite bourgeoisie?
(a) Middle-middle class people (b) Those who subscribe to traditional morality and the hierarchy of classes (c) Tradespeople and whitecollar workers (d) Conservative and reactionary class

217. At one time the front wheel of the bicycle used to be directly powered by pedals, and it used to be much larger than the rear wheel — hence the popular name Penny Farthing. When did both the wheels get to be of the same size, the rear wheel being powered by a sprocket chain drive?
(a) 1885 (b) 1901 (c) 1906 (d) 1911

218. What is a mugwump?

(a) A defector (b) An undecided person sitting on the fence, his mug on one side and his wump on the other (c) A cad (d) A politically neutral person

219. What does acumen mean?

(a) Acquired capacity (b) Mental keenness (c) Tendency (d) Knowledge

220. Of the following authors who has been translated more often and in more languages all over the world?

(a) Shakespeare (b) Charles Dickens (c) V.I. Lenin (d) Hans Chriastian Andersen

Quiz 12

221. Along with *perestroika*, the other reform initiated in the USSR by Gorbachev is *glasnost*. What is it?

(a) Freeing the stifled voice (b) Breaking down separationist barriers (c) Ending cultural isolationism (d) Acceptance of some cultural values of the capitalist West

222. During the Vietnam war Da Nang, a city in east Vietnam, was much written about. Why?

(a) It was the scene of frequent encounters between the government troops and the Viet Cong (b) It was the pleasure city for U.S. soldiers on short leave (c) It was the first major Vietnamese city to fall to the Viet Cong (d) It was the site of a huge U.S. military base

223. Quasars are quasi-stellar objects, the most distant and the most luminous objects in the universe, which are receding from our galaxy at speeds of 80% of the speed of light. They are probably 8 billion light years away. The fact that they can be spotted at all makes their luminosity equal to 100 galaxies combined. Digest this information and tell which one is the brightest quasar known to date.

(a) 3C-273 (b) XL-981 (c) QC-192 (d) OP-92
224. There is an instrument which can even measure the intensity of pain. What is it called?
(a) Algometer (b) Achimeter (c) Poinemeter (d) Penstetho
225. In which play does the stage direction occur: Exit, pursued by a bear?
(a) Samuel Beckett: *Waiting for Godot* (b) Sheridan: *Rivals* (c) Beaumont and Fletcher: *Philaster* (d) Shakespeare: *Winter's Tale*
226. Chanakya, an expert on government, was the principal adviser of a king, and so great was his influence on the king that one of the contemporary sources says that the king was a weak and insignificant young man and the real ruler of the empire was Chanakya. Who was the king?
(a) Chandragupta Maurya (b) Pushyamitra Sunga (c) Chandragupta II (d) Samudragupta
227. Which historical event is commemorated by the Marathon runs? The first runner was, of course, the messenger who brought the news of a Greek victory all the way to Athens, running.
(a) King Cyrus capturing Babylon (b) Persian attack on Athens defeated by Greece (c) Hannibal defeating the Romans at Marathon (d) Alexander defeating the Persians
228. Of these four capital cities, which is the most populous?
(a) London (b) New York (c) Moscow (d) Paris
229. In a particular country 35 million people still live in caves. Where?
(a) Borneo (b) The continent of Africa (c) China (d) Java
230. *Tabula rasa*, or a blank tablet, is how a philosopher described the state of human mind at birth. Who?
(a) Jeremy Bentham (b) John Locke (c) John Stuart Mill (d) George Berkeley

231. Gnosticism is a philosophical and religious system of ideas which
(a) believes in God, but denies the existence of Heaven (b) holds that salvation is only possible through individually revealed knowledge (c) neither believes nor disbelieves in the existence of God (d) is prepared to believe in God if someone can prove logically that God exists

232. What is gynaecomastia?
(a) Female sterility (b) Ovarian cyst (c) Flat chest in females (d) Enlarged male breast

233. Of the following vitamins which one contains a trace of metal?
(a) C (b) D (c) B_{12} (d) E

234. Of the following orchestras which is the latest?
(a) New York Philharmonic Symphony (b) Vienna Philharmonic (c) Liverpool Philharmonic (d) Hallé

235. Measures to protect the flora and fauna of the world are now increasing with man's growing realization of their importance in the biosphere. Which species first received such international recognition?
(a) Carnivores (b) Fish (c) Birds (d) High altitude herbivores

236. The first noun word in many short dictionaries begins with aardvark, which is an animal. Which country has it and gave it its name?
(a) South Africa (b) Australia (c) Holland (d) Malaysia

237. The cave paintings of Ajanta were executed over a period of several centuries. When was the earliest cave, now known as Cave X, done?
(a) Fourth century B.C. (b) First century A.D. (c) Third century A.D. (d) Sixth century A.D

238. The Planning Commission prepares the nation's Five-Year plans, but whose approval is necessary before the plans can start?

(a) The Prime Minister, in consultation with a special subcommittee of the Parliament (b) Parliament (c) The Council of Ministers (d) The National Development Council

239. Conditioned reflex is a predictable psychological reaction to a particular stimulus in the environment. Who discovered it?

(a) Gregor Mendel (b) Sigmund Freud (c) Trofim Lysenko (d) Ivan Pavlov

240. What is the meaning of bumptious?

(a) Spirited (b) Confident (c) Uneven (d) Noisy and conceited

Quiz 13

241. What was the Watergate Scandal which led to President Nixon's resignation?

(a) A huge amount of kickback which the President received at a place called Watergate (b) A water supply project that went to a contracting firm in which the President's wife held a considerable share (c) The burglary at the Democratic Party head-quarters, known as Watergate (d) The President's secret liaison with a lady of pleasure named Lucille Watergate

242. Which of the following science research institutes was the first to be established? Sir C.V. Raman used to research here.

(a) Tata Institute of Fundamental Research, Bombay (b) Indian Association for the Cultivation of Science, Calcutta (c) Indian Institute of Science, Bangalore (d) Physical Research Laboratory, Ahmedabad

243. The heliocentric theory of planetary motion, which holds that the sun is motionless at the centre of the universe with the planets revolving round it, was first propounded by

(a) Claudius Ptolemius, popularly known as Ptolemy
(b) Nicholas Copernicus (c) Galileo Galilei
(d) Aryabhata

244. Who invented the poison gas, the decimal point, and the toilet paper?
(a) The Swedes (b) The French (c) The English (d) The Chinese

245. An employee of a bookselling firm, he pondered deeply over the popularity of a novelist and found that his novels were all written to a formula. When he had acquired a pretty good idea of the mix he left his job and set up as an author, and sure enough he too became a bestseller. Who is this intelligent author?
(a) Jack Higgins (b) James Hadley Chase (c) Robert Ludlum (d) Harold Robbins

246. Although Indian archaeology was a relatively late field of interest among British scholars, the study of Indology started even during the Governor-Generalship of Warren Hastings. Who was the father of Indology?
(a) Charles Wilkins (b) Sir William Jones (c) H.H. Wilson (d) Henry Colebrooke

247. During which king's reign did Guy Fawkes try to blow up the British Parliament?
(a) Henry IV (b) Henry VIII (c) Elizabeth I (d) James I

248. Which country in the world has the largest deposit of uranium?
(a) Niger (b) South Africa (c) USA (d) Namibia

249. Which Indian crop earns the greatest amount of foreign exchange?
(a) Cotton (b) Tea (c) Groundnuts (d) Sugarcane

250. Princess Damayanti was so desirable as a bride that as many as four gods were present at the *swayamvara*, all looking like Nala, whom she had decided to

marry. Four clues told her who were not Nala. Choose one of clues from the following.

(a) The false Nalas did not sweat (b) The eyeballs of the false Nalas were not moving (c) There was a halo behind the head of each of the false Nalas (d) They were all looking a little bit anxious

251. Penicillin was first used in hospitals in India after World War II. When did Sir Alexander Fleming discover it?

(a) 1928 (b) 1932 (c) 1937 (d) 1941

252. A living organism has a number of minerals in its body, varying in quantity. Which mineral exists in the smallest quantity in the human body?

(a) Iron (b) Zinc (c) Copper (d) Manganese

253. What is the offspring of a mule called?

(a) Foal (b) Hinny (c) Milly (d) The question is stupid, for everyone knows that mules are sterile

254. Of the following books by John Le Carré, which is Smileyless?

(a) *Smiley's People* (b) *A Small Town in Germany* (c) *A Murder of Quality* (d) *Call for the Dead*

255. Which is the oldest surviving bookshop in India?

(a) Newman's in Calcutta (b) Higginbotham's in Madras (c) The Strand in Bombay (d) Das Gupta & Co., Calcutta

256. Who introduced prohibition for the first time in India?

(a) Morarji Desai (b) C. Rajagopalachari (c) Lal Bahadur Shastri (d) Gulzarilal Nanda

257. Which is the most ancient Indian treatise on astrology?

(a) *Ganitadhyay* by Bhaskaracharya (b) *Suryasiddhanta* by an unknown author (c) *Brihatsamhita* by Varahamihira (d) *Panchasiddhantika* by Varahamihira

258. Any idea what Zhonghua Renmin Gongheguo is?

(a) The Snow Leopard (b) A dish of fried termites (c) The Roof of the World (d) People's Republic of China

259. What is a person when you call him pussilanimous? (You shouldn't really use these hard words when simple synonyms are available)

(a) Cowardly (b) Ready to take offence at the slightest pretext (c) Ready to do physical violence at the slightest pretext (d) Extremely tight with his money

260. Give the meaning of debonair.

(a) Smart (b) Stylish (c) Well-dressed (d) Refined

Quiz 14

261. What is a Putsch, an occurrence frequent during Hitler's reign?

(a) Rapid conquest of a country (b) Forcible takeover of a government (c) Takeover of another country with the active help of Party infiltrators (d) A conquest

262. Who was the first scientist or philosopher to propound the theory of the atom?

(a) Mocritus (b) Leucippus (c) Kanada (d) John Dalton

263. The Sahitya Akademi has a provision for appointing Honorary Fellows. There is currently (till 1990) only one such foreign Fellow, and he is a distinguished poet. Can you name him?

(a) Günter Grass (b) Brian Patten (c) Leopold-Sedar Senghor (d) Joseph Brodsky

264. Who holds the Test record for the largest number of captaincy?

(a) Imran Khan (b) Clive Lloyd (c) W.G. Grace (d) Greg Chappell

265. In which Japanese martial art it used to be the object to pierce the opponent's skin?

(a) Judo (b) Jujitsu (c) Karate (d) Kendo

266. Pogrom, which literally means 'like thunder', is violent, government-condoned and sometimes government-assisted, attack on the Jews, once particularly virulent in countries like Poland, Germany, Russia, and other east European countries. Which language is the donor of the word?
(a) Germany (b) Russia (c) Hungary (d) Poland

267. Which is the world's oldest railway station?
(a) Victoria (b) Osaka (c) Liverpool (d) Leningrad

268. Which river flows through all these countries in Europe: Germany, Austria, Czechoslovakia, Hungary, Yugoslavia, and Romania?
(a) Rhine (b) Elbe (c) Oder (d) Danube

269. What is hedonism?
(a) The concept that the body's pleasures take precedence over the mind's (b) The concept that pain must be avoided at all costs (c) The notion that the mind and the body are one, hence the body's pleasures are the mind's (d) The principle that happiness is the sole and proper aim of human action

270. The people who attended Buddha's first sermon became his original disciples. How many were they?
(a) 5 (b) 7 (c) 21 (d) 30

271. If at a certain stage of pregnancy a woman has German Measles she is strongly advised to medically terminate her pregnancy, as the baby may have serious defects at birth. Which is that stage?
(a) Months 1-3 (b) Months 7-9 (c) Months 6-8 (d) At any stage

272. Who painted *The Last Supper*?
(a) Rembrandt (b) Leonardo da Vinci (c) Michaelangelo (d) Raphael

273. Rudyard Kipling, who was born in India, wrote a number of jungle tales which still remain popular. About which region did he write?

(a) Sunderbans (b) Ranthambore (c) Kanha
(d) Kumaon
274. When one reads about migration of animals between continents, one often comes across the terms New World and Old World. What is the New World?
(a) All the landmass outside Asia (b) Australia (c) Europe (d) North and South America
275. A bunch of schoolboys find themselves stranded in an island and very soon they turn themselves into absolute little devils. Which Nobel Prize winning author's vision of human nature is this?
(a) Camile Jose Cela (b) Joseph Brodsky (c) William Golding (d) Gabriel Garcia Marquez
276. The Andaman and Nicobar are a group of islands, and it was in Port Blair's notorious cellular jail that many of India's freedom fighters wasted away their lives. How many islands are there in the group?
(a) 37 (b) 113 (c) 231 (d) 223
277. Indian Railways have a number of long-haul passenger trains which can take one from one corner of the country to another. Which of the following performs the longest journey?
(a) Calcutta-Bombay Mail, via Allahabad (b) Frontier Mail (c) Guwahati-Trivandrum Express (d) New Delhi-Trivandrum Express
278. What is double jeopardy?
(a) Great danger (b) Two different kinds of danger (c) Doubled financial risk (d) Being prosecuted for the second time for the same offence
279. A pass can be bought from Indian Railways for unlimited travel over a period of time. What is it called?
(a) Indorail (b) See India (c) Indrama (d) Indrail
280. What is the meaning of abnegation?
(a) Refusal (b) Denial (c) Self-denial (d) Neglect

Quiz 15

281. Shuttle diplomacy is a fairly recent phenomenon in international relations. Which American President's name is associated with it?
(a) John F. Kennedy (b) Lyndon B. Johnson (c) Richard M. Nixon (d) Jimmy Carter

282. In which planet in our solar system are the days and nights the longest?
(a) Venus (b) Mars (c) Mercury (d) Pluto

283. *Desire under the Elms* was originally written as a play. It was made into a film in which Sophia Loren played a lead·role. Who wrote the play?
(a) Eugene O'Neill (b) Arnold Wesker (c) Tennessee Williams (d) Jean Cocteau

284. When was swimming first introduced in the Olympic Games?
(a) 1896 (b) 1904 (c) 1908 (d) 1912

285. In which country did skiing originate?
(a) Norway (b) Sweden (c) Finland (d) Switzerland

286. Between which dates was the American Civil War fought?
(a) 1848 and 1857 (b) 1851 and 1856 (c) 1871 and 1875 (d) 1861 and 1865

287. Which is the largest island in the world?
(a) Madagascar (b) Britain (c) Greenland (d) New Guinea

288. Which is the world's largest wine-producing country?
(a) Italy (b) France (c) Germany (d) Spain

289. Which is the longest river in Asia?
(a) Yangtse (b) Indus (c) Brahmaputra (d) Mekong

290. Which is the shortest of the Gospels?
(a) Matthew (b) Mark (c) Luke (d) John

291. Which of the following land measurements in acres would be closest to 100 hectares?
(a) 157 acres (b) 204 acres (c) 225 acres (d) 247 acres

292. Many of the sculptures of Parthenon in Athens are to be seen in the British Museum, because one Lord Elgin simply picked them up and shipped them to England, for a tidy profit. Who was the sculptor?

(a) Phidias (b) Praxiteles (c) Callicrates (d) Ictinus

293. Which animal is in the logo of the World Wide Fund for Nature (formerly World Wildlife Fund)?

(a) Teddy Bear (b) Giant Panda (c) Sloth Bear (d) Tiger

294. Which animal can hang upside down from branches of trees even when sleeping?

(a) The dingo (b) The sloth (c) The jaguar (d) The chimpanzee

295. 'Will you come upstairs, Dr. Watson, and inspect my collection of lepidoptera?'

Dr. Watson is there; therefore it must be a Sherlock Holmes story. Which?

(a) The Hound of the Baskervilles (b) The Adventure of the Speckled Band (c) The Sign of Four (d) A Study in Scarlet

296. India's Green Revolution brought about a dramatic increase in the production of wheat within a short span of time in the mid-sixties. Which scientist's name is associated with this achievement?

(a) Sir J.C. Bose (b) Dr. B.P. Pal (c) M.S. Swaminathan (d) N.S. Randhawa

297. When was the Communist Party of India born?

(a) 1921 (b) 1923 (c) 1925 (d) 1927

298. When W.H. Auden wrote his poem 'Homage to Clio' he was paying tribute to the Muse of a particular subject. What was Clio Muse of?

(a) Poetry (b) Friendship (c) History (d) Sculpture

299. What is a parvenu?

(a) A pimp (b) A flatterer (c) An upstart (d) A servile person

300. What is the meaning of asperity?
(a) Desperation (b) Sharpness of temper (c) Clarity
(d) Unequal status

Quiz 16

301. From 1950 to 1967 India's name occurred most frequently among the famine-stricken countries of the world. Since 1968 another country has usurped the position. Which?
(a) Nigeria (b) Bangladesh (c) Niger (d) Ethiopia
302. Which is the year of the first manned space flight?
(a) 1961 (b) 1963 (c) 1964 (d) 1965
303. Although it has been the fashion for half a century now to prefer realism to romanticism in literature, whenever a starkly realistic piece of writing has been produced people have given it a derogatory brand name. When in 1958 a play called *A Taste of Honey* was produced at the Theatre Royal, it was hailed as a landmark in the school of 'Kitchen Sink' realism. Who was the dramatist?
(a) Arnold Wesker (b) Shelagh Delaney (c) John Osborne (d) Terence Rattigan
304. Which events comprise a triathlon?
(a) Javelin throw, discus throw, and hammer throw (b) 5000m, 10,000m and 20,000m run (c) Long jump, high jump and pole vault (d) Long distance swimming, cycling, and running
305. Heinrich Himmler was perhaps the most dreaded among the Nazi leaders, and not the least of his claim to notoriety was his execution of 'the Final Solution' in which at least six million Jews were exterminated in the gas chambers. What happened to him finally?
(a) Sentenced to life imprisonment, he died in jail (b) On the day of Hitler's suicide he escaped, and

was never traced (c) He was sentenced to death in the Nuremberg trials and was hanged (d) He tried to escape, was arrested by the British, but committed suicide

306. According to the Moslem tradition, after Adam was expelled from the Garden of Eden he came down to the earth and settled in an island. Which?

(a) Madagascar (b) Crete (c) Sicily (d) Sri Lanka

307. It is mainly the revenue from oil that makes many African countries rich. To which country in sub-Saharan Africa does oil confer the highest per capita income?

(a) Gabon (b) Nigeria (c) Ghana (d) Upper Volta

308. Which is the capital of Pakistan-held Kashmir?

(a) Gilgit (b) Abbottabad (c) Muzaffarabad (d) Sopur

309. One of Nirad C. Chaudhuri's books is *The Continent of Circe*. Circe was an enchantress in Greek mythology who

(a) induced lethargy in men (b) turned men into sheep (c) turned men into swine (d) induced total forgetfulness in her victims.

Mr. Chaudhuri's *Continent* is India.

310. What are aphakic eyes?

(a) Eyes with crossed vision (b) Extremely shortsighted eyes (c) Eyes with damaged retina (d) Eyes from which the lenses have been removed, as after cataract operations

311. Which among the following forms of Greek classical architecture predates the others?

(a) Doric (b) Ionic (c) Corinthian (d) Hellenistic

312. The most important role that biotechnology will play in the future is likely to be in the area of:

(a) pollution control (b) waste treatment (c) food production (d) meeting energy needs

313. Which animal remains blind for eleven weeks after its birth?

(a) Mouse (b) Cat (c) Platypus (d) Armadillo

314. Arrange the following classical dramatists in chronological order.
(a) Aeschylus (b) Aristophanes (c) Euripides (d) Sophocles

315. Who wrote India's National Anthem?
(a) Sumitranandan Pant (b) Sarojini Naidu (c) Mahadevi Verma (d) Rabindranath Tagore

316. The *vidushaka*, the fool of Sanskrit drama, amiable but gluttonous, always a figure of fun, invariably belonged to one caste. Which?
(a) Brahman (b) The warrior caste (c) The trader caste (d) Sudra

317. A booby trap is one in which an unsuspecting person falls; hence a booby is a fool. Where is the word derived from?
(a) A large stupid animal found in Ghana (b) An antelope in the Saharan deserts which has no sense of danger (c) A gullible sea bird easily hunted (d) An Australian aborigine unacquainted with the civilized world, and therefore easily exploited

318. What is acrophobia?
(a) Fear of gymnastic exercises (b) Fear of large cities (c) Fear of heated controversy (d) Fear of great heights

319. What is a centurion?
(a) One who has made a score of a hundred (b) A Roman senator representing a hundred citizens (c) A Roman army officer commanding a hundred soldiers (d) One who has lived a hundred years or more

320. Which country won the World Cup football finals in 1986?
(a) West Germany (b) Argentina (c) Brazil (d) Italy

Quiz 17

321. The Cultural Revolution in China was launched by Chairman Mao Tse-Tung to revive the nation's

revolutionary spirit and to wage war against the 'bourgeois elements' in the cultural world and the bureaucracy. Can you remember when it started?

(a) 1956 (b) 1966 (c) 1961 (d) 1971

322. During which years was America's Vietnam war fought?

(a) 1961-68 (b) 1963-70 (c) 1965-73 (d) 1968-75

323. Who was the creator of MANIAC, the computer that made the hydrogen bomb possible?

(a) Leo Szilard (b) Niels Bohr (c) John von Neumann (d) Otto Hahn

324. Not many people have been awarded both the major literary prizes of the country. Can you name an Assamese author who has been honoured by both the Sahitya Akademi and the Bharatiya Jnanpith Foundation?

(a) Birendra Kumar Bhattacharya (b) Hiren Gohain (c) Chandrakanta Gogoi (d) Hitesh Deka

325. Who has scored a record of 49 goals for England in the World Cups?

(a) Frank Buckley (b) Bobby Collins (c) Bobby Charlton (d) Billy Wright

326. Which game was invented by the British army in India on a rainy afternoon?

(a) Billiards (b) Snooker (c) Ping Pong (d) Fencing

327. Which Roman emperor was the first to embrace Christianity and is regarded as the founder of the Christian empire?

(a) Augustus (b) Constantine I (c) Constantine IV (d) Maximilian I

328. Which is the widest waterfall in the world?

(a) Khone, Laos (b) Niagara, Canada (c) Victoria, Zimbabwe and Zambia (d) Seward, Peru

329. In which modern State would King Solomon's Mines be situated?

(a) Botswana (b) Ethiopia (c) Syria (d) Israel

330. *Angst,* or anguish, is felt by the modern man in an increasing magnitude. What is its philosophical cause?

(a) As mankind grows older, its knowledge of suffering increases (b) There is nothing to be done about bringing a change in one's future (c) One must freely choose one's actions to give a direction to one's undetermined future (d) The utter futility of living dawns upon man and yet he finds no avenues of escape

331. Which of the following is a basic concept common to Hinduism, Buddhism, and Jainism?

(a) Dharma (b) Karma (c) Nirvana (d) Kama

332. Normal human weight is related to height. By how much should one exceed that to be called fat?

(a) 50% (b) 35% (c) 20% (d) 10%

333. Western music scores are written on five parallel lines. What are those called?

(a) Staves (b) Quintets (c) Bars (d) Strings

334. In which year did the Bhopal gas disaster, in which methyl isocyanate gas leaked from a Union Carbide plant, killing and maiming hundreds, occur?

(a) 1981 (b) 1982 (c) 1983 (d) 1984

335. Which of the following birds cannot fly?

(a) Peahen (b) Platypus (c) Kiwi (d) Tern

336. Who wrote the first true encyclopedia?

(a) Vincent of Beauvais: *Mirror of the World* (b) Ephraim Chambers: *Cyclopaedia* (c) Pliny the Elder: *Natural History* (d) Diderot *et al* : *Encyclopedia*

337. The Ganga basin is the largest in India. What percentage of India's total land area does the Ganga drain?

(a) 25% (b) 30% (c) 33% (d) 40%

338. *Dashakumaracharita* is a collection of tales of ten princes, written in prose. Who was the author?

(a) Bana (b) Dandin (c) Subandhu (d) Kalidasa

339. What is an open-end investment company?

(a) One which has no limit to its share capital (b) One whose shares can be bought from the stock market (c) One which invests its funds in stock market shares only (d) One which invests only in safe government securities

340. What was Cinderella's coach made of?
(a) Egg shells (b) Glass (c) Pumpkin (d) Gourd

Quiz 18

341. The poet W.H. Auden, although averse to marriage, nevertheless did marry the daughter of a famous Jew to help her escape from Nazi Germany. Whose daughter?
(a) Sigmund Freud (b) Thomas Mann (c) Albert Einstein (d) Isaac Bashevis Singer

342. How long was the Long March (1934-35) under the leadership of Mao Tse-Tung (to use the more familiar form of his name)?
(a) 10,000 miles (b) 6000 miles (c) 3000 miles (d) 5000 miles

343. Cybernetics, a new branch of science developed by Norbert Weiner is a study of
(a) the best possible control of inventory, i.e., a firm's raw materials and stock of goods (b) the most economical utilization of a firm's resources, financial, human, and material (c) industrial or work procedures to determine the most efficient methods of operation (d) control systems in electronic and mechanical devices and comparisons between man-made and biological devices.

344. From which mineral is aluminium extracted?
(a) Bauxite (b) Feldspar (c) Lignite (d) Gypsum

345. Perhaps Shakespeare didn't like dogs. There is only one dog in his plays, but that too is set in a foreign country. Name the play.

(a) *Twelfth Night* (b) *Two Gentlemen of Verona* (c) *Taming of the Shrew* (d) *Titus Andronicus*

346. Who was the earliest Saint who had come to India to convert people to Christianity?
(a) St. Francis Xavier (b) St. Thomas (c) St. Columba (d) St. Bartholomew

347. Who made this sad comment on man's social and intellectual conduct?

> Let us honour if we can
> The vertical man
> Although we value none
> But the horizontal one.

(a) W.H. Auden (b) Boris Pasternak (c) Pablo Neruda (d) Philip Larkin

348. In which of the following countries does nuclear power supply 20% of the country's electricity requirement?
(a) France (b) Sweden (c) Finland (d) USSR

349. Which country in the world was the first to grow coffee?
(a) India (b) Brazil (c) Congo (d) Abyssinia

350. At the end of the present dark age, *kali*, Hindu legends say that Vishnu will appear in one of his incarnations to destroy the evil and bring succour to the virtuous. In what form will he appear?
(a) The Man-Lion, or Narasimha (b) The Boar, or Varaha (c) Kalki, or a man mounted on a white horse with a flaming sword in hand (d) Rama, who will establish an order of justice and virtue

351. What are the statistical chances of giving birth to twins?
(a) 1 to 1.4% (b) 2.2 to 2.5% (c) 2.5% (d) 1.6%

352. Placebo (pronounced pla-si-bo) is a pharmaceutical product administered to a certain kind of patients. Which?

(a) Those suffering from terminal illness (b) AIDS victims (c) Hypochondriacs (d) Those suffering from diseases of love

353. What is Jackson Pollock famous in the United States as?

(a) A dramatist (b) A poet (c) A country music singer (d) Abstract expressionist painter

354. The presence of one of the following in household effluents is fatal to freshwater life. Name which.

(a) Detergents (b) Wood ash (c) Phenyle (d) Oily substances

355. The Pinkheaded Duck is now an extinct species in one country. Which?

(a) India (b) China (c) England (d) Siberia

356. Who was awarded the first Sahitya Akademi prize for English?

(a) Khushwant Singh (b) R.K. Narayan (c) Raja Rao (d) A.K. Ramanujan

357. Among the States in India which one has kept the population growth under the greatest control?

(a) Haryana (b) Rajasthan (c) Kerala (d) Tamil Nadu

358. When did Mahatma Gandhi return to India from South Africa to give leadership to her struggle for independence?

(a) 1915 (b) 1918 (c) 1921 (d) 1922

359. What is the difference between a crown and a coronet?

(a) No difference. Both words are derived from Latin *corona* (b) A coronet is larger than a crown (c) A crown is entirely made of gold, whereas a coronet has gems studded in it (d) A crown is worn by a king, whereas a coronet is worn by a nobleman

360. What is the meaning of miscegenation?

(a) Mismatching (b) Interbreeding of races (c) Marrying someone from a lower caste (d) Marrying one's close relatives

Quiz 19

361. The Gang of Four, a term of strong political diapproval, consisted of Jiang Quing, Wang Hongwen, Yao Wenyuan, and Zhang Qunqiao. What did they earn notoriety for?
(a) Embezzling party funds (b) The excesses of the Cultural Revolution (c) Conspiring with the CIA to overthrow the Communist regime (d) Advocating the formation of a bourgeois elite

362. Cockpit flight recorders became a compulsory instrument in commercial aircraft as late as
(a) 1967 (b) 1972 (c) 1960 (d) 1969

363. One of the epics of the Tamil people is the *Ramayanam*. Who wrote it?
(a) Anonymous (b) Kamban (c) Thiruttakkadevar (d) Avvaiyar

364. In which game is the Thomas Cup awarded?
(a) Rugby (b) Tennis (c) Badminton (d) Baseball

365. Who held the world chess title between 1975 and 1985?
(a) Boris Spassky (b) Bobby Fischer (c) Anatoly Karpov (d) Viktor Korchnoi

366. What finally happened to Field Marshal Rommel, the Desert Fox of the North African war in World War II?
(a) He was killed in action at Al Alamein (b) He fell into the hands of the British, who kept him imprisoned during the war, but released him afterwards (c) He was tried at the War Crimes Trial at Nuremberg, but found not guilty (d) He was accused of plotting against Hitler's life and was forced to take poison

367. Which country in the world has large deposits of all the following minerals: bauxite, chromium, copper, iron, lead, manganese, nickel, tin and zinc.
(a) Canada (b) Australia (c) USSR (d) China

368. In which country is more than 50% of the world's cork produced?

(a) France (b) Spain (c) Portugal (d) Italy

369. The greatest happiness principle holds that the supreme good is the greatest happiness of the greatest number. Of which philosophy is it the basic tenet?

(a) Utilitarianism (b) Marxism (c) Idealism (d) Indian Materialism

370. Even Lord Buddha had some enemies, and one of them continued his enmity throughout Buddha's life, persecuting his disciples. Who was he?

(a) Devadatta (b) Ajatashatru (c) King Prasenjit (d) Chanda Pradyot

371. There are altogether four blood groups: A, B, AB, and O. Which of these is known as the universal donor?

(a) A (b) B (c) AB (d) O

372. In which country was Leonardo da Vinci, the painter of *Mona Lisa*, born?

(a) France (b) Italy (c) Holland (d) Belgium

373. 'Overkill' may wipe out the existence of man on earth. What is it?

(a) Overexploitation of the soil to leave it ultimately barren (b) Overindustrialization, causing total atmospheric pollution, choking mankind to death (c) Overuse of pesticides killing all animal life in the long run (d) Use of the entire nuclear stockpile in the world, wiping out life on earth thirteen to fourteen times over

374. Among animals which has the longest gestation period?

(a) Rhinoceros (b) African elephant (c) Blue whale (d) Camel

375. In banning of authors the Soviet Union has perhaps done one better than Nazi Germany; it is often difficult to understand why. In 1929 the Soviet

Union banned an English author for 'occultism and spiritualism'. Can you guess who?

(a) Emily Bronte (b) Bram Stoker (c) W.B. Yeats (d) Sir Arthur Conan Doyle

376. The ancient Hindu lawgiver, Manu, was traditionally hard on women. What punishment did he prescribe for a woman taken in adultery — with a person of lower caste?

(a) Her ears should be publicly cut off (b) She would be condemned to live as an ostracized widow for the rest of her life (c) She would have to pay to ten Brahmins the money value of ten fecund cows (d) She should be torn apart by dogs

377. As early as 1938, Jawaharlal Nehru became Chairman of the National Planning Committee which was constituted at the instance of the Indian National Congress. When Nehru became Prime Minister of a free India, naturally national planning became one of his priorities. When did the government appoint the Planning Commission?

(a) 1947 (b) 1949 (c) 1950 (d) 1951

378. How is the vanilla flavour obtained?

(a) Through a synthetic process (b) Through a special treatment of sugar (c) From the bark of a tree (d) From a special kind of orchids

379. Anniversary gifts rise in value with the rise in the number of years. What gift should you give on someone's first wedding anniversary?

(a) Paper (b) Cotton (c) Glass (d) Plastic

380. What is the meaning of the Anglo-Indian word gentoo?

(a) A native gentleman (b) A Bengali baboo (c) A highly educated native (d) A Hindu as opposed to a Moslem

Quiz 20

381. The game theory is now extensively used to calculate the best possible strategies in gamelike situations such as war, business, and politics. It holds that when deciding on a course of action in a situation of conflict one must predict the course of action of the opponent, knowing at the same time that the opponent is engaged in the same exercise. Who is the originator of the theory?

    (a) Wolfgang Pauli (b) John von Neumann (c) Milton Friedman (d) Simon Kuznets

382. Of the following layers of atmosphere which lie above the earth's surface, which is the highest?

    (a) Troposphere (b) Ionosphere (c) Mesosphere (d) Stratosphere

383. A child who will speak English has to learn the poem 'Twinkle, twinkle, little star'. Who wrote it?

    (a) Ann Taylor (b) Jane Taylor (c) Ann and Jane Taylor (d) Lewis Carroll

384. Vinson Massif, 16,860 ft/5140m is in

    (a) Nepal (b) Tibet (c) The Swiss Alps (d) Antarctica

385. When did Muhammad Ali reign as the World Heavyweight Boxing champion?

    (a) 1961-64 (b) 1964-67 (c) 1962-65 (d) 1963-67

386. Thermopylae is a pass which, in ancient times, was an entrance into Greece from the north. In 480 B.C. a great battle was fought there. Between whom?

    (a) The Greeks and the Spartans. The Greeks lost
    (b) The Spartans and the Turks. The Spartans won
    (c) The Greeks and the Slavs. The Greeks won
    (d) The Spartans and the Persians. The Spartans lost

387. The Riviera is a fashionable Mediterranean resort area in southern Europe. In which country is Monte Carlo?

    (a) Spain (b) France (c) Monaco (d) Italy

388. What is the capital of Australia?

(a) Sydney (b) Canberra (c) Melbourne
(d) Adelaide
389. Tradition has it that the sage Vyasa composed the *Mahabharata*. Who was his scribe?

(a) Ganesha (b) Sarasvati (c) Narada (d) Vedavati
390. What should be the daily quantity of urine production in a healthy body?

(a) 1 litre (b) 1.5 litres (c) 2 litres (d) 2.2 litres
391. Of the following bowed string instruments which is the smallest?

(a) Violin (b) Viol (c) Violoncello (d) Double Bass
392. The global temperature is now at a critical level. If it falls by a certain degree the Ice Age will engulf the earth. By what degree?

(a) 4°C (b) 5°C (c) 10°C (d) 2°C
393. Among the birds which can fly which is the heaviest?

(a) Emu (b) Peafowl (c) Great Indian Bustard
(d) Kori Bustard
394. Few people have read the book *Small Is Beautiful*, yet the use of the phrase is widespread, and advertising copywriters and people who are fond of catch phrases use it about anything small, from a car to a business enterprise. Who wrote this book which advocates the use of a technology in tune with the environment?

(a) Alvin Toffler (b) Vance Packard (c) E.F. Schumacher (d) John von Neumann
395. India is a petroleum importing country. How much of its petroleum needs is met by local production?

(a) 30% (b) 47% (c) 58% (d) 70%
396. By which year has the Government of India vowed to achieve universal elementary education, and eradication of illiteracy in the 15-35 age group?

(a) 1995 (b) 2001 (c) 2005 (d) 2010
397. In which year did Sir C.V. Raman receive the Nobel prize for Physics?

(a) 1930 (b) 1932 (c) 1936 (d) 1931

398. Trinity, Magdalen, Jesus, Pembroke — to which University do these colleges belong?

(a) Harvard (b) Oxford (c) London (d) Cambridge

399. What does recondite mean?

(a) Difficult (b) Requiring special knowledge to be understood (c) Meaningless (d) That which makes a compromise between two contradictory points of view

400. What is the chief ingredient of the Dutch dish, coleslaw?

(a) Ham (b) Cabbage (c) Chicken liver (d) Cucumber

Quiz 21

401. A quisling is a traitor to his country, who delivers it to the invading army. The real Quisling was a Fascist who helped Germans conquer his country. After the war he was tried for treason and shot. Which country did he belong to?

(a) France (b) Denmark (c) Norway (d) Austria

402. What would 100°C be in the Fahrenheit?

(a) 132° (b) 180° (c) 212° (d) 196°

403. *Madhushala*, a contemporary Hindi epic poem, has been recently published in a new translation, seeking a larger readership. Who is the poet?

(a) Maithili Sharan Gupta (b) Harivanshrai Bachchan (c) Mahadevi Verma (d) Jaishankar Prasad

404. In which year was the world's most prestigious tennis championship, Wimbledon, started?

(a) 1877 (b) 1893 (c) 1901 (d) 1905

405. Which cricketer was a practising gynaecologist?

(a) Len Hutton (b) Sonny Ramadhin (c) W.G. Grace (d) Polly Umrigar

406. The U.S. Declaration of Independence is considered to be the most important of all American

historical documents and one man wrote it almost entirely. Who?

(a) George Washington (b) Alexander Hamilton (c) Aaron Burr (d) Thomas Jefferson

407. Which waterfall in the world is the highest, i.e., by drop from lip to base?

(a) Victoria, Upper Yosemite (b) Ribbon Fall, USA (c) Angel Falls, Venezuela (d) Wollomombi, Australia

408. To which country do the Galapagos Islands, famous for Darwin's voyage to them, belong?

(a) Costa Rica (b) Ecuador (c) Colombia (d) Panama

409. In logic different kinds of arguments are described. What is *argumentum ad baculum*?

(a) Argument appealing to a rational human being (b) Argument of the cudgel (c) Argument appealing to respect (d) Argument appealing to ignorance

410. The first English translation of the *Bhagavad Gita* (1784) from the original Sanskrit was done by

(a) Sir William Jones (b) Charles Wilkins (c) Henry Colebrook (d) Horace Hayman Wilson

411. What should be the duration of a full-term pregnancy?

(a) Ten months (b) Nine months (c) 280 days (d) 287 days

412. Which is the home of the Kuchipudi dance?

(a) Andhra Pradesh (b) Tamil Nadu (c) Karnataka (d) Kerala

413. Vedic literature speaks of a life-giving, life-supporting system on earth. Which of the following is it?

(a) River (b) Earth (c) Rain (d) Air

414. What is kosher fish? Kosher food is that which is in accordance with Jewish dietary laws.

(a) Fish with scales and fins (b) Fish without scales (c) Fish cooked in milk (d) Fish which live on weeds only

415. Which was the first one-volume general encyclopedia in English?
(a) *Chambers General Encyclopedia* (b) *Oxford World
Encyclopedia* (c) *Random House World Encyclopedia*
(d) *Columbia Encyclopedia*
416. For which international meet was Vigyan Bhavan
used for the first time?
(a) India hosting a UNESCO conference (b) India
hosting the Non-Aligned Heads of States Conference (c) A meeting of the International Monetary
Fund (d) A meeting of eminent scientists of the
world to discuss nuclear disarmament
417. Which is the most ancient script of India?
(a) Brahmi (b) Kharoshthi (c) Grantha (d) Deva-
nagari
418. The University of California has nine campuses.
Which is its main campus?
(a) Berkeley (b) Los Angeles (c) Santa Barbara
(d) San Francisco
419. What is pulchritude?
(a) Fatness (b) Amorous tendency (c) Physical
beauty (d) Generosity
420. What is a connoisseur?
(a) A lover of good things of life (b) An art expert
(c) An expert on food (d) A person with an expert
knowledge in some particular field

Quiz 22

421. Of the following Concentration Camps established
by the Nazis, which accounted for the most deaths?
(a) Auschwitz (b) Belzec (c) Majdanek
(d) Treblinka
422. The theory of organic evolution posits that life on
earth began as a simple protoplasmic mass from
which arose, in course of time, all living forms. Who

conducted the first experiment that proved that life on earth could be the result of chemical evolution?
(a) Barbara McClintock (b) Susumu Tonegawa (c) Stanley L. Miller (d) Konrad Lorenz

423. Peace and quiet are what married men most value in their homes, and, of course, lots of love. Someone offered this fail-safe prescription:

> To keep your marriage brimming
> With love in the marriage cup,
> Whenever you're wrong, admit it;
> Whenever you're right, shut up.

— Who is the author of this?
(a) Hillaire Belloc (b) W H. Auden (c) Ogden Nash (d) Lord Byron

424. The ancient Olympic Games began in Greece in 776 B.C., but gradually fell into disfavour and were discontinued at the end of the fourth century A.D. When did the modern revival of the Games take place?
(a) 1888 (b) 1892 (c) 1896 (d) 1900

425. Where did the game basketball originate?
(a) Japan (b) Malaysia (c) USA (d) Mexico

426. One of the most important amendments to the U.S. Constitution, Amendment XV, was passed to give equal rights to all Americans, irrespective of race, creed, or colour. It also prohibited discrimination on the grounds of previous enslavement. What is the date of the amendment?
(a) 1865 (b) 1870 (c) 1885 (d) 1940

427. Which is the oldest university town in Europe?
(a) Heidelberg in Germany (b) Sorbonne in Paris (c) Bologna in Italy (d) Salzburg in Austria

428. Which is the most populous State in the United States of America?
(a) New York (b) New Jersey (c) Florida (d) California

429. Which among the following countries does not belong to the United Arab Emirates?

    (a) Dubai (b) Sharjah (c) Kuwait (d) Abu Dhabi

430. This lady of Greek mythology was endowed with the gift of prophecy, but fated never to be believed. Who?

    (a) Persephone (b) Cassandra (c) Hermes (d) Medea

431. Name the largest gland of the body.

    (a) The thyroid gland (b) The pituitary gland (c) Liver (d) The adrenaline gland

432. In a typical seating plan of a symphony orchestra, which instruments are closest to the conductor's podium?

    (a) Horns (b) Clarinets and bassoons (c) Violins (d) Trumpets and trombones

433. When heat is trapped on the surface of the earth by atmospheric pollution we have the greenhouse effect, which gradually raises the temperature on the earth's surface. Which pollutant is mainly responsible?

    (a) Carbon dioxide (b) Carbon monoxide (c) Ozone (d) Sulphur dioxide

434. Which is the longest-living animal in the world?

    (a) Elephant (b) Tortoise (c) Bison (d) Whale

435. *The Great Railway Bazaar*, one of the train travel classics, describes the author's journey from the Victoria Station in London to Tokyo Central, and back to London through Burma, India, Iran, Turkey, and central Europe, travelling in as many as thirty railway lines. Who is the author?

    (a) Lawrence Van der Post (b) Paul Theroux (c) Eric Newby (d) Jonathan Raban

436. When did the practice of decennial census start in India?

    (a) 1861 (b) 1881 (c) 1901 (d) 1911

437. What with publications in various regional languages and not the least in English, India is a fairly large

producer of books (although how many produced are sold in the end is anybody's guess). What would be her world ranking?

(a) Third (b) Fourth (c) Sixth (d) Seventh

438. Of the Nobel Prizes in various subjects which has been shared by two or more persons more times than the others?

(a) Physics (b) Chemistry (c) Physiology or Medicine (d) Literature

439. What have Sheraton, Hepplewhite, and Queen Anne in common?

(a) All designs of china (b) Varieties of cheese (c) All chair designs (d) All apples

440. What is a parquet floor?

(a) Multicoloured mosaic (b) Covered with cork (c) Covered with wall-to-wall carpet (d) Covered with pieces of hardwood fitted in a pattern

Quiz 23

441. USA, UK, France, and USSR have the power of the veto in the United Nations. Which other country has it?

(a) Japan (b) China (c) Switzerland (d) India

442. Electric lamps are sealed after they are filled with this gas. Identify which.

(a) Argon (b) Oxygen (c) Helium (d) Hydrogen

443. In Calcutta's Park Street cemetery lies the remains of an English girl loved by an English poet, whose poem, 'Rose Aylmer' ends with these lines:

> Rose Aylmer, whom these wakeful eyes
> May weep, but never see,
> A night of memories and sighs
> I consecrate to thee.

— Who is the poet?

(a) Thomas Moore (b) W.S. Landor (c) Rudyard Kipling (d) George Meredith

444. The oldest golf club in India is the second oldest in the world after England. Where is it located?
(a) Bombay (b) Madras (c) Calcutta (d) Jaipur

445. How many referees are there in a wrestling bout?
(a) 1 (b) 2 (c) 3 (d) 4

446. Hiring goons to change the complexion of politics is nothing new; a recorded case goes back to the first century B.C. Who was the farsighted man, or woman, as the case may be?
(a) Octavius Caesar (b) Cleopatra, Queen of Egypt (c) Publius Clodius Pulcher (d) Caius Julius Caesar

447. On the banks of which river does Leningrad lie?
(a) Don (b) Volga (c) Neva (d) Dnieper

448. Central America is a collective term applied to six nations lying SE of Mexico. Which among the following nations is not Central American?
(a) Costa Rica (b) Colombia (c) Panama (d) Belize

449. Which South-east Asian country has never been colonized?
(a) Laos (b) Malaysia (c) Thailand (d) Kampuchea

450. What is the zodiacal sign Virgo represented by?
(a) Woman (b) Bull (c) Fish (d) Pair of scales

451. How many taste buds are there on the human tongue?
(a) Around 300 (b) Around 1000 (c) Around 2500 (d) Around 3000

452. Harold Pinter, who has been called by the *Times,* London, 'our best living playwright', wrote the screenplay of one of the following films. Which?
(a) *Schindler's List* (b) *Tess of the D'Urbervilles* (c) *The Third Man* (d) *The French Lieutenant's Woman*

453. Slums or shanty towns are a worldwide feature of the industrial civilization, although the worst are in Asia. Where is Asia's largest slum located?
(a) Shanghai (b) Calcutta (c) Saigon (d) Bombay

454. The presence of one of the following in cutlery may poison the system and ultimately cause cancer. Which?

(a) Tin (b) Nickel (c) Chromium (d) Lead

455. The cat family has small as well as large members. Which is the largest?

(a) Siberian Lion (b) African Lion (c) Siberian Tiger (d) Royal Bengal Tiger

456. Which Shakespearian play opens in a brothel in Vienna?

(a) *All's Well That Ends Well* (b) *Measure for Measure* (c) *Cymbeline* (d) *Pericles*

457. Mahabalipuram, or more properly, Mamallapuram, has a famous rock sculpture made under the Pallava kings. What is the subject of this sculpture?

(a) The temptation of the Buddha (b) Fighting bulls (c) The descent of Ganga (d) Vishnu rescuing the earth from the cosmic ocean

458. By the year 1990 India has registered a population growth of 2.1% per annum. If the trend continues, by a certain date India's population will overtake China's. Can you tell the date?

(a) 2010 (b) 2020 (c) 2030 (d) 2040

459. Nike shoes are now worn all over the world, including India. Does the name have any significance?

(a) Nike was the Greek goddess of victory (b) Nike was a Greek messenger, the fastest runner of his time (c) The word was made up of the name of its maker Nikos Esterhazy (d) It's a nonsense word

460. What is a freebooter?

(a) One who lives off charity (b) A person who shares in plunder without doing anything (c) A person who looks for free gifts when buying something (d) A person who lives from plunder

461. 'To right a wrong it is necessary to exceed proper limits, and the wrong cannot be righted without the proper limits being exceeded' — who said this?
    (a) Niccolo Machiavelli (b) V.I. Lenin (c) Josef Stalin (d) Mao Tse-Tung

462. The deficiency of which hormone causes cretinism?
    (a) Thyroid hormone (b) Adrenaline hormone (c) Pituitary hormone (d) Testoterone

463. Fifteen-year-old Alex and his three friends start an evening's mayhem by hitting an old man, tearing up his books and stripping him of his money and clothes, or, in Nadsat, the teenage argot of a not too future, Alex and his three droogs tolchok an old veck, razrez his books, pull off his outer platties and take a malenky bit of a cutter. Who wrote this chilling novel?
    (a) Kathy Acker: *Blood and Guts in High School* (b) Samuel Beckett: *More Pricks than Kicks* (c) Ernest Hemingway: *Men without Women* (d) Anthony Burgess: *A Clockwork Orange*

464. The first Olympic Game in 776 B.C. was confined to only one event. What was it?
    (a) Running (b) Wrestling (c) Javelin throw (d) Archery

465. In which sport, since its inception as a competition event, have the blacks dominated the whites?
    (a) Long jump (b) Baseball (c) Boxing (d) Long distance running

466. This Ivan justly earned the sobriquet 'the Terrible'. In a rage he killed his son, created a special terror police called the *oprichniki*, and married seven times, disposing of his wives by ordering them to take the veil or ordering their murder. Which Ivan was this?
    (a) Ivan III (b) Ivan IV (c) Ivan V (d) Ivan VI

467. Which is the largest volcano in the world?
(a) Mt. Kilimanjaro (b) Mt. Vesuvius (c) Mt. Etna
(d) Mt. Krakatoa

468. Which explorer made the largest number of expeditions to Antarctica, five?
(a) Roald Amundsen (b) R.F. Scott (c) Richard E. Byrd (d) R.E. Peary

469. In which city in India was the first medical college started?
(a) Calcutta (b) Patna (c) Allahabad (d) Bombay

470. How did King Pandu die in the *Mahabharata*?
(a) He died of leprosy (b) He was killed by the demon Tarakasura (c) He died under a curse while cohabiting with his wife Madri (d) He was bitten by the serpent Takshaka during his self-exile in the forest

471. What disease is myocardial infarction?
(a) Stoppage of urine (b) Breathlessness (c) Chronic chest pain (d) Heart attack

472. Until the age of 35 this famous painter was a stockbroker. Within five years he painted *The Yellow Christ*, now in the Albright-Knox Gallery in the United States. Little recognized in his lifetime, he died in poverty. Whose story is this?
(a) Paul Cezanne (b) Paul Gauguin (c) Vincent Van Gogh (d) Edouard Manet

473. When was the Wildlife (Protection) Act, offering succour to the endangered species of India, passed?
(a) 1972 (b) 1976 (c) 1968 (d) 1971

474. Which creature of the animal kingdom should man be most afraid of?
(a) Mosquito (b) Common housefly (c) Cockroach (d) Snake

475. Whose pen-name was Elia?
(a) Oscar Wilde (b) Charles Lamb (c) Charlotte Bronte (d) G.K. Chesterton

476. The Kumbha Mela is held every twelve years alternately in four places. Haridwar and Prayag are well known. Which are the other two places?
(a) Varanasi (b) Ujjain (c) Nasik (d) Sagar Island

477. The foundation of the National Park System was laid by the U.S. Congress in 1872. Which is the oldest National Park in the USA?
(a) Yellowstone National Park (b) Yosemite National Park (c) Grand Canyon National Park (d) Mount Rainier National Park

478. Which drink is called Mother's Ruin?
(a) Rum (b) Gin (c) Absinthe (d) Brandy

479. What does inchoate mean?
(a) Confused (b) Undeveloped (c) Inseparably mixed (d) Inarticulate

480. In Kalidasa's *Meghaduta* a yaksha offends Kubera and is banished from his city of Alaka, in the Himalayas, to Ramgiri, for a year. Whereabouts would Ramgiri be?
(a) Uttar Pradesh (b) Madhya Pradesh (c) Himachal Pradesh (d) Orissa

Quiz 25

481. What is the Irangate Scandal, the name imitating the Watergate scandal?
(a) The U.S. President's secret negotiations with Iran for the release of U.S. hostages (b) Selling Iran nuclear secrets by the USA for a tidy sum of money (c) Supplying Iran with strategic arms by the USA secretly (d) The buying by the USA of Iranian oil through a third country

482. Where in the world was the first atomic power station built?
(a) France (b) USA (c) England (d) USSR

483. Of the following Nobel Prize winners, who was the first ever to win the prize for Physics?

(a) W.C. Roentgen (b) Philipp Lenard (c) Marie S. Curie (d) Pierre Curie

484. The first ever formulation of a theory of evolution was by

(a) Pliny the Elder (b) Alfred Russel Wallace (c) Jean Lamarck (d) Charles Darwin

485. A novel of sex and psychiatry, *The Fear of Flying*, created quite a sensation in the United States, where it was first published, as late as 1973. Who is the author?

(a) Germaine Greer (b) Philip Roth (c) Erica Jong (d) Susan Howatch

486. Since Britain's split with Rome most British monarchs have been Church of England. Who is Britain's last Roman Catholic king?

(a) James I (b) James II (c) William III (d) William IV

487. Gods and goddesses had different names in Greek and Roman. Who is the Roman counterpart of the Greek goddess Hera, the wife of the supreme god?

(a) Diana (b) Juno (c) Minerva (d) Vesta

488. Among the oil-producing countries which tops the list?

(a) Nigeria (b) Saudi Arabia (c) Iran (d) Russia

489. Which is the largest desert in the world?

(a) Gobi (b) Sahara (c) Kalahari (d) Great Victoria

490. Which book of the Old Testament was composed first?

(a) Matthew (b) Mark (c) Luke (d) John

491. The founder of the Eugenics Movement was John Galton, cousin of Charles Darwin. Eugenics holds

(a) that the Aryan races are basically superior to non-Aryan races (b) that by carefully manipulating the surroundings and following a particular educational programme, it is possible to make an average child a genius (c) that the unfit should be discouraged from propagating, a view welcomed by the Nazis (d) that talent is inherited, rather than imported

492. *The Hay Wain* is one of the most famous landscape paintings in the world. Who painted it?
(a) Claude Lorrain (b) Jacob van Ruysdale (c) Van Gogh (d) John Constable

493. Benvenuto Cellini (1500-1571) is called by the historians of the times as a true renaissance man who attained distinction in many fields. However, he became mostly famous as a
(a) statesman (b) painter (c) poet (d) jeweller

494. Among human beings it is difficult to say whether monogamy, polygamy, or polyandry is really the common mating habit. Among animals which is the most common mating system?
(a) Monogamy (b) Polygamy (c) Polyandry (d) Polygyny (i.e., mating with more than one female during the mating season)

495. In which novel, to keep the citizens on the strait and narrow path, do signs in public places proclaim 'Big Brother is watching you'?
(a) *1984* (b) *Darkness at Noon* (c) *Animal Farm* (d) *Gulag Archipelago*

496. The bicycle industry in India is doing very well, exporting the machines to the USSR and Europe. In which city or town is the industry concentrated?
(a) Salem in Tamil Nadu (b) Sonepat in Haryana (c) Ludhiana in Punjab (d) Vadodara in Gujarat

497. The Tata Iron and Steel Company (TISCO), started by J.N. Tata, is India's largest and most prosperous steel plant. When was its first steel mill built?
(a) 1896 (b) 1903 (c) 1907 (d) 1912

498. Piracy, which is robbery on the high seas, flourished until the late nineteenth century. The following are some famous pirates, with one fictitious character. Identify him.

(a) Sir Francis Drake (b) Blackbeard (c) Captain Flint (d) Captain Kidd

499. What is the correct term for a she-ass?
(a) Slut (b) Mare (c) Hinny (d) Jenny

500. What is the meaning of abrogate?
(a) Surrender (b) Repeal (c) Take by force (d) Deny

Quiz 26

501. Where is the International Atomic Energy Commission, a specialized agency of the U.N., located?
(a) Vienna (b) Paris (c) Geneva (d) Ottawa

502. One of the following astronauts was a pilot in the first space shuttle flight. Who?
(a) Joe Engle (b) Oleg Atkov (c) Edwin Aldrin (d) Neil Armstrong

503. Guy de Maupassant, French short story writer, wrote a very large number of stories, novels, plays, sketches in his short 43-year-old life, and exerted a tremendous influence on English and European Literatures. Which set of dates pertain to him?
(a) 1842-1885 (b) 1850-1893 (c) 1864-1907 (d) 1870-1913

504. Who can compete in the Special Olympic Games?
(a) Mentally retarded persons (b) Persons above 60 years of age (c) Convicts serving life sentences (d) Third World countries

505. Which game is played in such English pubs as have not been tarted up?
(a) Chinese Checkers (b) Darts (c) Contract bridge (d) Chess

506. Of the following Brutuses, who killed Julius Caesar?
(a) Lucius Junius Brutus (b) Marcus Junius Brutus (c) Caius Longinus Brutus (d) Decimus Junius Brutus

507. Paper was manufactured in Europe 1500 years after it was in this country:

(a) Egypt (b) Mexico (c) India (d) China

508. What has the ancient Russian city Nizhni Novgorod been rechristened as?

(a) Stalingrad (b) Leningrad (c) Gorki (d) Petrograd

509. Potato was introduced from the New World into the Old. From which place did it come?

(a) West Virginia in America (b) Peru (c) Chile (d) Mexico

510. At the end of the Kurukshetra war only ten among the Pandavas and Kauravas were left alive. How many were there of each?

(a) Seven Pandavas and three Kauravas (b) Eight Pandavas and two Kauravas (c) Nine Pandavas and one Kaurava (d) There were no Kaurava survivors

511. To which part does the strongest muscle of the human body belong?

(a) Thighs (b) Hips (c) Pelvis (d) Jaw

512. With the gradual depletion of natural sources, it will be increasingly necessary to exploit non-conventional energy sources. Which is the fuel of the future?

(a) Methane (b) Hydrogen (c) Recycled flammable waste (d) Argon

513. This rare animal used to be found in India till 1947, when it was hunted to its extinction. What is it?

(a) The Giant Panda (b) The Black Himalayan Bear (c) The Snow Leopard (d) The Ibex

514. The Greenhouse Effect written about recently by ecologists is

(a) the greening of the earth as a result of conservation programmes (b) the trapping of heat on the surface of the earth by the atmosphere (c) vegetation attracting moisture from the atmosphere, leading to further vegetative growth (d) the effect of trapped temperature in a closed space promoting certain types of plant growth

515. In which famous book does the servant Passepartout appear?

(a) *Don Quixote* (b) *Round the World in Eighty Days* (c) *Winnie the Pooh* (d) *Vanity Fair*

516. *Brighter than a Thousand Suns*, which C.P. Snow said, is 'by far the most interesting historical work on the atomic bomb I know of', was written by

(a) Robert Oppenheimer (b) Robert Jungk (c) Norbert Wiener (d) Hermann Weyl

517. The birth of the Indian cinema was with the feature film *Raja Harishchandra*, made by Dadasaheb Phalke. Which year was it?

(a) 1910 (b) 1913 (c) 1917 (d) 1921

518. Press censorship isn't just a symptom of totalitarianism; as a curb on the freedom of expression it has been practised for a long time. When did it begin in India?

(a) 1799 (b) 1818 (c) 1857 (d) 1885

519. What is the meaning of obsequious?

(a) Obvious (b) Mourning (c) Arrogant (d) Attentive in a servile manner

520. What is the meaning of adventitious?

(a) Exciting (b) Accidental (c) Laborious (d) Lucky

Quiz 27

521. Henry Kissinger, President Nixon's political adviser, called Bangladesh a basket case. What he meant was that

(a) the problems of Bangladesh can't be considered piecemeal but have to be taken as a whole (b) Bangladesh is a basketful of economic, social, and political problems (c) Bangladesh empties its population among the neighbouring countries like an upturned basket (d) Bangladesh has problems which defy any solution

69

522. An astronomical unit is the distance between the earth and the sun. It is
(a) 92,960,000 km (b) 192,690,000 km
(c) 149,604,970 km (d) 291,069,000 km

523. Bharatiya Jnanpith was founded to promote the literatures in the Indian languages, and every year a substantial award is made to the best writing in any one of the Indian languages. Who was the founder of Bharatiya Jnanpith?
(a) Lala Shriram (b) Sahu S.P. Jain (c) G.D. Birla (d) J.R.D. Tata

524. Who does the colourful term 'tomato can' describe?
(a) A clumsy baseball player (b) An amateur tennis player (c) A fat, blundering footballer (d) A clumsy boxer

525. At what height are the baskets hung in basketball?
(a) 7'6" (b) 8' (c) 10' (d) 8'6"

526. Who was the first Roman emperor?
(a) Tiberius (b) Pompey (c) Julius Caesar (d) Augustus

527. In which country lies the largest deposit of tin?
(a) Bolivia (b) China (c) Indonesia (d) USSR

528. How many States in the USA have a city named Moscow?
(a) 7 (b) 8 (c) 9 (d) 10

529. What is incontinence in philosophical parlance?
(a) Weakness of memory (b) Weakness of will (c) Weakness of the rational faculty (d) The inability to hold on to a conviction

530. In the *Mahabharata* the story is told of a king who had 100,000 wives, and the wives bore him 1,000,000 sons. Each of his sons married 100 wives, and each wife received, as her dowry, 100 each of elephants, bulls, horses, milch cows, lambs, and goats. You do not have to count the total number of animals given as dowry; just identify the king.
(a) Shakalya (b) Shrutasena (c) Sasabindu (d) Shala

531. Which blood group does one have to have to accept
the blood of any of the four groups?
(a) A (b) B (c) AB (d) O

532. Mendelssohn composed incidental music for a
Shakespearian play. Which is it?
(a) *Romeo and Juliet* (b) *Twelfth Night* (c) *Othello* (d) *A
Midsummer Night's Dream*

533. Provision of a green belt is given great importance
in modern town planning. What is a green belt?
(a) Adequate plantation in the city area to absorb
atmospheric pollution (b) Creation of avenues by
planting trees on the roadside (c) Afforested areas
in the periphery of towns and cities (d) Pockets of
semi-rural, low-density population scattered around
a city

534. What speed can the fastest bird in the world,
white-throated spine-tailed swift, reach?
(a) 110 kmph (b) 130 kmph (c) 160 kmph (d) 170
kmph or above

535. Lexicographers, i.e., dictionary makers, are trained
to make fine distinctions of meaning between words
which may seem to us synonymous. This
lexicographer's wife caught him kissing the cham-
bermaid. 'Why, soandso, I'm surprised,' she ex-
claimed. He pointed out, severely, 'Madame, *you* are
astonished, *I* am surprised'. Who is he?
(a) Sir James Murray (b) Noah Webster (c) A.S.
Hornby (d) Professor John Sinclair

536. Which is the longest river in India?
(a) Ganga (b) Brahmaputra (c) Godavari (d) Sone

537. The Howrah-Delhi Rajdhani Express used to be the
fastest train in India, completing the 1440 km
journey in seventeen hours. Recently, however, it
was outstripped in speed by another train. Name
which.
(a) Pandyan Express (b) Delhi-Bombay Rajdhani Express (c) Shatabdi Express (d) Taj Express

538. Which is the oldest university in Germany?
    (a) Gottingen (b) Freiburg (c) Heidelberg (d) Leipzig
539. Crown Derby, Spode, Swansea — what kind of thing are these names of?
    (a) Horses (b) Apples (c) Cattle (d) China
540. What is an al fresco lunch?
    (a) Sharing pot luck with others (b) A buffet lunch (c) Open-air lunch (d) Fixed price, but eat-as-much-as-you-can lunch

Quiz 28

541. Which country has the largest armed force relative to the size of its population?
    (a) Pakistan (b) North Korea (c) Iran (d) Vietnam
542. Which was the year of man's first setting his foot on the moon?
    (a) 1963 (b) 1965 (c) 1969 (d) 1971
543. Most John Le Carré fans make it a point to read all his books, and rightly so, because he is such a delightful writer. His earlier books, however, are not very easy to get. Which is the earliest?
    (a) *The Looking-Glass War* (b) *A Murder of Quality* (c) *A Small Town in Germany* (d) *Call for the Dead*
544. How many holes are there in a standard golf course, which is usually 5.5 km in length?
    (a) 12 (b) 18 (c) 16 (d) 21
545. With which sport is the term regatta associated?
    (a) Horse racing (b) Motor car racing (c) Rowing (d) Polo
546. Who was the ruler of Palestine at the time of the crucifixion of Jesus?
    (a) Antipater (b) Herod the Great (c) Herod Antipas (d) Caligula
547. Which island did Ganguin's paintings make famous?
    (a) Tahiti (b) Samoa (c) Cook Islands (d) Pago-Pago

548. Antarctica, the continent on the South Pole, was first reached by an explorer in 1911 (14 December). Who was the explorer?
(a) Roald Amundsen (b) R.F. Scott (c) Richard E. Byrd (d) R.E. Peary

549. In which city was the first modern astronomical observatory built in India?
(a) Darjeeling (b) Shillong (c) Madras (d) Pune

550. Draupadi of the five husbands was also called Panchali, i.e., the woman from Panchala. What is Panchala now?
(a) Uttar Pradesh (b) Bihar (c) Himachal Pradesh (d) Punjab

551. What is diuretics?
(a) Medicine which helps increase the blood pressure in low-pressure patients (b) Medicine which induces one to vomit (c) Medicine which helps urine production (d) Medicine which relieves constipation

552. Which fish is generally released into water for biological control of mosquito larvae?
(a) Carp (b) Tilapia (c) Hilsa (d) Minnows

553. Which animal is known to have the highest known metabolic rate and must eat incessantly to keep alive?
(a) Mouse (b) Shrew (c) Hare (d) Mole

554. Who lived at 83 Clevedon Terrace?
(a) Betjeman's Miss Joan Hunter-Dunn (b) Macavity the Mystery Cat (c) Dr. Watson (d) Auden's Miss Edith Gee

555. Small employers are often known to run several separate work units rather than combine them into one, to prevent the workers from forming trade unions. What is the minimum number of workers needed to form a trade union according to the Indian Trade Union Act of 1926?
(a) 7 (b) 10 (c) 12 (d) 14

556. In 1990 the world population is estimated to be 5.3 billion, and it keeps multiplying. Demographers however predict that global population will stabilize after it has reached a certain figure. What is it?
(a) 8.5 billion (b) 10.2 billion (c) 12 billion (d) 14.6 billion

557. How long did Prohibition last in the USA, barring, of course, widespread bootlegging (term derived from the practice of smugglers of actually concealing the bottles inside their high boots)?
(a) 1869-1897 (b) 1911-1921 (c) 1919-1933 (d) 1927-1935

558. What is a poltergeist?
(a) A bonding agent (b) Universal consciousness (c) A knocking ghost (d) A chicken coop

559. What is chalcedony?
(a) Bearing false witness (b) Uttering heresies (c) A gem stone (d) An alloy

560. What is the correct meaning of bland?
(a) Without salt and spices (b) Dull and uninteresting (c) Smooth (d) Pleasing

Quiz 29

561. An important German philosopher of this century announced his conversion to Hitler's National Socialism in a public address in 1933, and distanced himself from his former Jewish teacher. Who is this National Socialist?
(a) Edmund Husserl (b) Martin Heidegger (c) Karl Jaspers (d) Leo Baeck

562. How far from the earth is the nearest star, apart from the sun? The star is Proxima Centauri.
(a) 23 light years (b) 13 light years (c) 6.3 light years (d) 4.22 light years

563. 'I never read any novels except my own. When I feel worried, agitated or upset, I read one and find

the last pages soothe me and leave me happy'. How marvellous would it have been if most novelists could follow this practice. Who is this extremely popular novelist?

(a) Jaqueline Susan (b) Barbara Cartland (c) Barbara Bradford Taylor (d) Harold Robbins

564. Decathlon, an Olympic event since 1912, is a combination of ten field and track events. Which among the following events does not feature in it?

(a) Discus (b) Javelin (c) Marathon (d) High jump

565. In which country did golf originate?

(a) Austria (b) Scotland (c) Switzerland (d) England

566. Which Louis was the king of France at the time of the French Revolution and was guillotined by the Convention?

(a) Louis XIV (b) Louis XV (c) Louis XVI (d) Louis XVIII

567. To which country does the volcano Cotopaxi belong?

(a) Ecuador (b) Mexico (c) Honduras (d) Chile

568. After Paris, which is the world's largest primarily French-speaking city?

(a) Berne (b) Oran (c) Saigon (d) Montreal

569. Which active volcano, the highest in Europe, lies in the island of Sicily?

(a) Vesuvius (b) Etna (c) Stromboli (d) Krakatoa

570. In Hindu mythology when the gods moved about they used their mounts, and most of them had their distinctive mounts, rarely sharing them with others. In one case, however, Sarasvati's mount, swan, was also used by another god. Who?

(a) Yama (b) Indra (c) Brahma (d) Kama

571. How much urine accumulates in the bladder of a normal person per minute?

(a) 1 ml or more (b) 3 ml or more (c) 5 ml or more (d) 8 ml or more

572. Sir John Vanbrugh was a Restoration period dramatist, whose best-known plays are *The Relapse* and *The Provoked Wife*. He was also a gifted architect. What did he build?

(a) The Blenheim Palace (b) The Buckingham Palace (c) The Windsor Palace (d) Saint Paul's Cathedral

573. A particular country liquidated its tiger population as being harmful to agricultural and pastoral occupations. Which is it?

(a) USSR (b) China (c) Brazil (d) Israel

574. Which bird is the world's longest distance flier?

(a) Arctic Tern (b) Siberian Crane (c) Siberian Duck (d) Alpine Swift

575. Whose detective is Father Brown?

(a) Agatha Christie (b) Erle Stanley Gardner (c) G.K. Chesterton (d) Marjorie Allingham

576. Alexander the Great, in his invincible march of conquest through India, was forced to turn back after he had reached the banks of a certain river. Which was it?

(a) Indus (b) Ravi (c) Beas (d) Jhelum

577. Besides subsidizing the publication of textbooks so that they can be made available at a low enough price, the N.B.T., or the National Book Trust publishes a large number of books, again at quite low prices, for children and in Indian languages. When was it set up?

(a) 1949 (b) 1953 (c) 1957 (d) 1961

578. One of the following won the Nobel Prize twice, in the unlikely combination of the subjects of Chemistry and Peace. Identify.

(a) Albert Einstein (b) Frederick Sanger (c) Konrad Lorenz (d) Linus Pauling

579. If you are holding your opponent in a half nelson what kind of combat are you in?

(a) Judo (b) Wrestling (c) Karate (d) Jujitsu

580. What is the meaning of misapprehend?
    (a) Misunderstand (b) Arresting the wrong person
    (c) Fearing something or some event unnecessarily
    (d) Miscalculate

Quiz 30

581. In order to make it impossible for the Viet Cong
    to hide in jungles the USA dropped huge quantities
    of this defolinant on Vietnamese vegetation. Apart
    from burning up jungles it brought disease and
    death to living creatures. Identify the chemical.
    (a) Nitroglycerine (b) Trinitrotoluene (c) Agent
    Orange (d) Thorium-X
582. The internal combustion engine, which has brought
    a tremendous change in human life and the environ-
    ment, was developed by
    (a) Karl Benz (b) Gottlieb Daimler (c) Henry Ford
    (d) Vannever Bush
583. The Kodak camera was invented in 1888 by George
    Eastman, who was also the inventor of the process
    of colour photography. When was the process
    invented?
    (a) 1902 (b) 1921 (c) 1928 (d) 1931
584. Galapagos Islands, an archipelago of several islands
    on the Pacific, derive their importance from the fact
    that
    (a) Captain Cook set foot on it and was murdered
    by the natives (b) it was first discovered by Magellan
    (c) the Hydrogen bomb was detonated here to test
    its destructive potential (d) it is an archipelago where
    much wildlife is to be found arrested at various
    evolutionary stages
585. Quite a few novelists and literary critics have written
    on the art of fiction, but perhaps one came closest
    to the mark when he wrote, 'There are three rules

for writing a novel. Unfortunately, no one knows what they are'. Who is this novelist?

(a) W. Somerset Maugham (b) Virginia Woolf (c) E.M. Forster (d) Kingsley Amis

586. Which British king ascended the throne at the age of ten?

(a) Edward VI (b) Aethelred (c) Edward IV (d) William IV

587. What is the region of origin of the very English tree, Elm?

(a) Japan (b) Southern Europe (c) North America (d) England

588. Which explorer discovered the West Indies?

(a) Vasco da Gama (b) Christopher Columbus (c) Captain Cook (d) Sir Francis Drake

589. Which country in Asia has the largest railway network?

(a) India (b) China (c) Japan (d) Burma

590. When was the Authorized Version of the Bible, also known as the King James Version, published?

(a) 1605 (b) 1609 (c) 1611 (d) 1616

591. What is an antigen?

(a) It is a virus or bacterium or some foreign substance which invades the body (b) It is an antibody which fights with hostile bacteria (c) It is an immunity-destroying virus (d) It is a chemical which can alter the genetic structure.

592. Marguerite Duras, an eminent French novelist, has also written screenplays and directed films. Which among the following is her screenplay?

(a) *Last Year in Marienbad* (b) *Hiroshima mon amour Gigi* (c) *Wild Strawberries* (d) *All Fall Down*

593. What do a lion, a lynx, a tiger, and a cheetah share in common?

(a) They are all gregarious animals (b) All inhabit the forests of India (c) They are all man-eaters (d) They are all members of the cat family

594. Among the following novels by Salman Rushdie, which one was his earliest?
(a) *Midnight's Children* (b) *Grimus* (c) *Shame* (d) *Satanic Verses*

595. Which city in India has the largest population?
(a) Calcutta (b) Bombay (c) Delhi (d) Madras
(Actually the choice is between the first two; the others are merely included as fillers)

596. The first power-driven jute mill was established in 1859, when the British had barely recovered from the Sepoy Mutiny. Where was it located?
(a) Chittagong (b) Dacca (c) Rishra (d) Manchester

597. What does the Gresham's Law state?
(a) Bad money drives out good (b) When the annual inflation rate goes to two digits economic depression follows almost immediately (c) Subsidy by the State to any particular industry always cripples its efficiency (d) Restricting money supply will always raise the price of gold

598. 'Anybody who hates children and dogs can't be all bad' — who said that?
(a) Oscar Wilde (b) Mark Twain (c) W.C. Fields (d) George Bernard Shaw

599. What is the meaning of lugubrious?
(a) Vast and unwieldy (b) Clumsy (c) Excessively mournful (d) Unbalanced

600. Woolworth's stores are well-known for their cheap, but often reliable goods — almost anything one would expect to find in a departmental store. At what prices did the first Woolworth store in Lancaster, Pennsylvania (1879), sell its goods?
(a) 5 cents, any item (b) 10 cents, any item (c) No price exceeding 10 cents (d) 5 and 10 cents

Quiz 31

601. In Japan a *zaibatsu* is a family-controlled banking and industrial combine, such as Mitsubishi, Mitsui, Sumitomo, and Yasuda. What does *zaibatsu* literally mean?
     (a) Money baron (b) Industrial giant (c) Money clique (d) Heavyweight

602. Where are the headquarters of the UNESCO?
     (a) New York (b) Paris (c) Geneva (d) Rome

603. In our solar system which planets have no satellites?
     (a) Neptune (b) Venus (c) Pluto (d) Mercury

604. How many light years is a parsec?
     (a) 3.26 light years (b) 4.83 light years (c) 5.25 light years (d) 10 light years

605. In which year was the Davis Cup international team competition started?
     (a) 1890 (b) 1897 (c) 1902 (d) 1900

606. Which Indian emperor was a patron and player of polo?
     (a) Babur (b) Sher Shah (c) Humayun (d) Akbar

607. What happened to the last Mughal emperor of Indi Bahadur Shah Zaffar, after the Sepoy Mutiny?
     (a) He was shot by Captain Hodson (b) He was arrested and imprisoned in the Red Fort till he died (c) He was exiled to the Andamans (d) He was exiled to Burma

608. Apart from the top ten mountains in Asia, which is the next highest?
     (a) McKinley (b) Aconagua (c) Pik Kommunizma (d) Mont Blanc

609. Where do the Blue Nile and the White Nile meet in great scenic splendour?
     (a) Cairo (b) Khartoum (c) Asmara (d) Giza

610. Of the bulk of Aristotle's writings which have more or less survived uncorrupted, which subject engaged

the most serious scholarly attention in the early middle ages?

(a) Logic (b) Metaphysics (c) Poetics (d) Ethics

611. She was so beautiful, loving, sweet, and such a delightful companion that the ten years that sage Vishwamitra spent with her seemed like a day. Who could be this dream of a celestial maiden?

(a) Urvashi (b) Rambha (c) Menaka (yes, this is the correct spelling of the name) (d) Tilottama

612. The human body grows at different paces at different periods of life. When is its growth fastest?

(a) Between ages 8 and 13 (b) Between ages 10 and 16 (c) Between ages 15 and 21 (d) Between ages 18 and 25

613. In Western music which is the queen of instruments?

(a) Violin (b) Organ (c) Trombone (d) Viola

614. Bodies of the dead are so commonly thrown into the Ganga in the belief that the holy river is the surest road to the 'Heavenly Abode' that an aquatic animal had to be released in its waters to get rid of the putrescent flesh. Name it.

(a) Turtle (b) Porpoise (c) Tilapia fish (d) Dolphin

615. Antelopes are known to be swift runners and great jumpers. A certain species of antelope is the highest (10 ft) and the longest (30 ft) jumper of them all. Which is it?

(a) Impala (b) Gazelle (c) Moose (d) Red Deer

616. The Folger Shakespeare Library, which happens to possess the largest number of copies of *The First Folio*, i.e., the first ever edition of the complete works of Shakespeare, is the largest repository of anything to do with Shakespeare. Where is it located?

(a) Cambridge, U.K. (b) Cambridge, Massachusetts (c) New York (d) Washington, D.C.

617. *Aryabhata*, the first Indian spacecraft, named after the ancient astronomer (whose name is often misspelt as Aryabhatta), was successfully launched in 1975. Which spacecraft followed next?
(a) *Aryabhata* II (b) *Bhaskara* (c) *Rohini* (d) *Dhruva*
618. What is dry wine, as distinguished from sweet wine?
(a) Dry wine has absolutely no water content (b) Dry wine has a relatively more alcoholic content (c) In dry wine the sugar has fermented completely (d) Dry wine is made from sun-dried grapes
619. What is the meaning of quizzical?
(a) Pertaining to quizzes (b) Doubtful (c) Strange (d) Questioning and mocking
620. What is the meaning of banal?
(a) Obscene (b) Blasphemous (c) Commonplace (d) Ugly

Quiz 32

621. The works of Aristotle, Shakespeare, and Dickens were banned in this country as corrupting. Finally, in 1968 the ban was lifted. Which country?
(a) China (b) Soviet Russia (c) Albania (d) East Germany
622. In the event of a nuclear holocaust a certain kind of energy will destroy all electronic devices anywhere. Which kind?
(a) Gamma radiation (b) Electronic pulse (c) Nuclear radiation (d) Intense heat
623. Meters are measuring devices and we are acquainted with various kinds. What does psychrometer do?
(a) It measures the loss of body heat in conditions of natural or induced cold (b) It records brain impulses in a sleeping person (c) It measures the moisture content of gases (d) It is a lie detecting device, measuring heartbeats when a question is asked

624. Who invented the pneumatic tyre?
(a) J.B. Dunlop (b) C. Goodyear (c) Robert Inchek (d) C. Magee

625. Jorge Luis Borges, author of *A Universal History of Infamy, The Book of Sand,* and *The Book of Imaginary Beings,* has greatly influenced a number of contemporary novelists, Salman Rushdie among them. Which country does he belong to?
(a) Argentina (b) Spain (c) Guatemala (d) Chile

626. The Aryans who invaded and settled in India had a mixed pastoral and agricultural economy. Which two animals were the most important to them?
(a) The cow and the bull (b) The goat and the sheep (c) The cow and the elephant (d) The cow and the horse

627. Where would you now try to find the remains of the ancient city of Carthage?
(a) Algeria (b) Tunisia (c) Madeira Island (d) Crete

628. What is the unit of currency in Spain called?
(a) Peso (b) Peseta (c) Centavo (d) Franc

629. Where is the world's largest airport?
(a) London (b) New York (c) Jedda (d) Dubai

630. When Draupadi became the wife of five husbands who had an equal share of her, her period of stay with each husband by rotation was decided. What was the period?
(a) One week (b) A fortnight (c) A month (d) A year

631. Lipids are important structural materials in living organisms. Their characteristic is that
(a) they multiply very fast (b) they are insoluble in water, but soluble in organic solvents (c) they are malign cells (d) they are the principal male hormone

632. Which is the largest of the following wind instruments?
(a) French Horn (b) Bassoon (c) Tuba (d) Trombone

633. Which among the following creatures is immune to snake poison?
(a) Buffalo (b) Mongoose (c) Eagle (d) Boar

634. The Russian poet of the Revolution, Vladimir Mayakovsky, who sang gloriously about it, became disenchanted with the Stalin era, and died shortly, at the age of 37 (1893-1930). How did he die?
(a) Shot in a purge (b) In Lubianka prison, insane (c) Committed suicide (d) Sent to Gulag for reformation, but caught tuberculosis there

635. Without *inquilab zindabad* hardly any political demo is complete. Who gave India the slogan?
(a) Khan Abdul Ghaffar Khan (b) Lala Lajpat Rai (c) Subhas Chandra Bose (d) Bhagat Singh

636. Who wrote the ancient treatise on polity, *Arthasastra*?
(a) Chanakya (b) Kautilya (c) Vishnugupta (d) Kumaradeva

637. A concordat is a formal agreement reached between
(a) the head of the Roman Catholic Church and the head of the State (b) two heads of different churches (c) the head of the Protestant Church and the head of the State (d) two heads of sovereign States

638. What is the meaning of uxorious?
(a) Miserly (b) Lecherous (c) Excessively attached to one's wife (d) Someone with a questionable past

639. What is the meaning of brown study?
(a) Melancholy (b) Tantrums (c) Deep thoughtfulness (d) Absentmindedness

640. In Britain what does the *Hansard* record?
(a) Peerage (b) International movement of ships (c) Postings of the clergy (d) Parliamentary proceedings

Quiz 33

641. Which country is the largest exporter of arms in the world?
     (a) USSR (b) USA (c) France (d) Sweden
642. Who was the very first person to walk on the moon?
     (a) Valentina Tereshkova (b) Neil Aldin Armstrong
     (c) Yuri Gagarin (d) John Glenn
643. John Barth is very funny American novelist. In one of his novels the hero is begotten by a computer. Which novel is it?
     (a) *Gravity's Rainbow* (b) *Q* (c) *The Player Piano*
     (d) *Giles Goat-Boy*
644. Which martial art was developed by the Japanese master Dr. Jigoro Kano?
     (a) Kendo (b) Jujitsu (c) Judo (d) Karate
645. In which country did the game of badminton first start?
     (a) India (b) Britain (c) China (d) Korea
646. Which calendar was the first to determine the days in the months as we know them, e.g., April, June, September, and November have 30 days, etc.?
     (a) The Julian calendar (b) The Gregorian calendar
     (c) The Jewish calendar (d) The Roman calendar
647. Which city is known as the Big Apple?
     (a) New York (b) Washington (c) Los Angeles
     (d) Florida
648. The New Territories, a mainland area of Hong Kong, was leased by the Chinese to the British for 99 years, late in the nineteenth century. When does the lease expire?
     (a) 1995 (b) 1996 (c) 1997 (d) 1998
649. The oldest central Asian city, and one of the world's oldest cities, it was known as the golden Samarkand, and so sacked by Jenghis Khan. Tamerlane made it his capital. To which embassy will you have to apply for a visa if you should wish to visit it?

(a) USSR (b) Iran (c) Iraq (d) Turkey

650. When Hindus die they are all expected to go to their 'Heavenly Abode', at least by their fond relatives. Where is it, this *vaikuntha*?

(a) Mount Kailasa (b) Sumeru (c) Mandar (d) Himalaya

651. Which vitamin is manufactured by ultraviolet radiation on the skin?

(a) A (b) B (c) D (d) E

652. The chief source of atmospheric pollution are emissions from industrial complexes and motor vehicles, which release a number of gases. In fact, in Nazi Germany gas vans were used to kill large batches of Jews. Which gas in these emissions is the most harmful?

(a) Carbon monoxide (b) Sulphur dioxide (c) Nitrogen monoxide (d) Carbon dioxide

653. Those who keep cats as domestic pets must have noticed that cats seem to spend most of the day and night sleeping, except when they are caterwauling. For how many hours in a 24-hour day does a cat sleep?

(a) 20 (b) 16 (c) 12 (d) Cats do not sleep all that much; since they enjoy most of their sleep during the day it looks as if they are inordinate sleepers

654. Who wrote the following poem:

'I am His Highness' Dog at Kew;
Pray tell me Sir, whose Dog are you?'

(a) Alexander Pope (b) Ben Jonson (c) Jonathan Swift (d) Lord Byron

655. Apart from dialects a large number of languages is spoken in India and the Eighth Schedule of the Constitution recognizes some as official languages. How many?

(a) 15 (b) 16 (c) 17 (d) 18

656. Of the following ancient mathematicians who was the earliest, preceding the others by at least four centuries?
(a) Aryabhata (b) Brahmagupta (c) Mahavira (d) Bhaskara

657. The Nobel Prizes for Chemistry, Physics, and Physiology or Medicine are always awarded to chemists, physicists, physiologists or medical researchers. The prize for Literature, however, has sometimes been given to philosophers and historians. Which of the following historians was awarded the Nobel Prize for Literature?
(a) Edward Gibbon (b) Theodor Mommsen (c) G.M. Trevelyan (d) Hugh Trevor-Roper

658. Which country has a totally unadorned, unpatterned, white flag?
(a) Ethiopia (b) Western Sahara (c) Haiti (d) Monaco

659. What is the meaning of egregious?
(a) Living in a herd (b) Travelling a lot (c) Outstandingly bad (d) Of a high standard

660. Who are the Hasidim?
(a) Reformed Jews who do not set much store by traditional religious observances (b) Orthodox Jews of Poland (c) Jewish priests (d) Jews who maintain the highest standard of religious observance and moral action

Quiz 34

661. Although exact figures are never published, estimates have been made about a country's expenditure on defence as a proportion of a country's Gross National Product; under 2% being low, and 10% being quite high. Among the following which are high spenders?
(a) Sri Lanka (b) Panama (c) Costa Rica (d) Laos

662. Which was the first ever manned space flight programme?
(a) Apollo: Command and Service Modules (b) Vostok (c) Voshkod (d) Gemini

663. On Midsummer Night supernatural beings were believed to roam the earth, and in Shakespeare's *A Midsummer Night's Dream* some pretty odd things happen. Which night is it?
(a) 21 June (b) 23 June (c) 24 June (d) 20 June

664. In which country is basketball the national game?
(a) Canada (b) Bahamas (c) USA (d) Hawaii

665. Which game is played for money in the square outside Harvard University, known as the Harvard Square?
(a) Poker (b) Chess (c) Chinese checkers (d) Ludo

666. The Industrial Revolution in Britain, which occurred between 1750 and 1850, was triggered off by the introduction of
(a) the use of coal as a source of power (b) the application of steam to obtain power (c) the introduction of the railways (d) the use of mechanized spinning machines

667. Which country invented playing cards, fishing reels, and whisky?
(a) Britain (b) France (c) China (d) The Indians of North America

668. What is the former African State of Nyasaland now called?
(a) Tanzania (b) Rwanda (c) Malawi (d) Gabon

669. Which is the oldest mountain range in India?
(a) Himalaya (b) Satpura (c) Nilgiri (d) Aravalli

670. The *apsaras* were born of one of the elements. Name which.
(a) Earth (b) Water (c) Wind (d) Fire

671. What do carbohydrates turn into when they are digested?
(a) Fats (b) Muscles (c) Blood (d) Glucose

672. Oil is one of the major pollutants of the sea; it spreads thinly over a very large surface and makes it impossible for marine creatures to breathe. Who invented the superbug to fight it?
(a) Charles Babbage (b) Vikram Sarabhai (c) Ananda Chakrabarti (d) Georg Wittig

673. Which, according to the Pahari lore, as reported by the late Desmond Doig, is the way to escape from a female yeti when attacked on the mountain?_
(a) Hide in the nearest crevice, for yetis can't see well (b) Run sideways, as the yeti has only a straight vision (c) The female yeti has a very heavy bottom, so one should run upwards (d) Run downwards, as the female yeti's speed will be hampered by her excessively pendulous breasts

674. What is the source of the title of the book *Tender Is the Night*?
(a) Shakespeare: *Romeo and Juliet* (b) Shelley: *Queen Mab* (c) Keats: *Ode to a Nightingale* (d) Shelley: *To Night*

675. When did Indian TV become colourful?
(a) 1978 (b) 1980 (c) 1982 (d) 1983

676. The *Aitareya Brahmana* describes one particular caste as 'paying tribute to another, to be lived upon by another, to be oppressed at will'. Which caste could it be so dismissive about?
(a) Brahman (b) The warrior class (c) The trader class (d) Sudra

677. What is Bonsai?
(a) Cultivation of dwarf trees and plants (b) Japanese martial art (c) Philosophy of self-contemplation (d) Japanese flower

678. 'A peasant must stand a long time on a hillside with his mouth open before a roast duck flies in'. Which country has this proverb?
(a) Japan (b) Thailand (c) China (d) Russia

679. What is the meaning of captious?

(a) Assertive (b) Loud-mouthed (c) Sudden
(d) Fault-finding
680. What is the zodiacal sign Capricorn also known as?
(a) The water bearer (b) The fish (c) The crab
(d) The goat

Quiz 35

681. The name of the aircraft which dropped the first atomic bomb on Hiroshima on 6 August 1945 was
(a) Marion Anderson (b) Lili Marlene (c) Enola Gay
(d) Marylin
682. This mathematician claimed that he solved maths problems through divine intervention. Who was he?
(a) Brahmagupta (b) Varahamihira (c) Ramanujan
(d) Pythagoras
683. What are binary stars?
(a) A pair of stars that lie along nearly the same line of sight from the earth but are not physically associated (b) Closely revolving stars which contain atoms of two different elements (c) Two associated stars revolving round a common centre of gravity
(d) Two horizontally close stars as seen through the telescope, maintaining a uniform speed.
684. Which articles of domestic use are covered with the solid, chemically inert polymer tetrafluoroethylene, or Teflon?
(a) Stainless aluminium utensils (b) Insides of pressure cookers (c) Non-stick frying pans (d) Insides of micro-wave ovens
685. MCC, or the Marylebone Cricket Club, as everyone knows, is the oldest cricket club in the world. Which is the world's second oldest?
(a) Sydney Cricket Club (b) Calcutta Cricket Club
(c) Oxford University Cricket Club (d) Union Cricket Club, Bombay

686. In the first ever World Cup Football which country defeated Argentina 4-2?

(a) Brazil (b) Uruguay (c) Mexico (d) Holland

687. Timur or Tamerlane made a bloody invasion of India and by his cruelty and rapacity distinguished himself as one of the worst invaders India has had. What is the date of his invasion?

(a) 1298 (b) 1340 (c) 1376 (d) 1398

688. Among the following airports which is the closest to London?

(a) Paris (b) Dublin (c) Brussels (d) Amsterdam

689. Which is China's most populous city?

(a) Beijing (b) Nanjing (c) Shanghai (d) Guangzhou (Canton)

690. There are traditional scholastic nicknames for many philosophers, and they are appropriately all in Latin. Thus the Miraculous Doctor, Roger Bacon, was *Doctor Mirabilis*; the Universal Doctor, Albertus Magnus, was *Doctor Universalis*; *Doctor Subtilis* the Subtle Doctor, was Duns Scotus. Who was *Doctor Angelicus*, or the Angelic Doctor?

(a) St. Augustine (b) St. Thomas Aquinas (c) Zeno of Elea (d) St. Bernard

691. Which among the *Puranas* is devoted to the Vaishnava religion and its rituals?

(a) *Vishnupurana* (b) *Bhagavatapurana* (c) *Naradiyapurana* (d) *Lingapurana*

692. Gallstones are sometimes formed in the gall bladder as a result of

(a) deposits of calcium in drinking water (b) taking fatty foods in excess (c) crystallization of bile (d) crystallization of acid produced in the stomach

693. Who made the highest ever runs in Test cricket at Lord's?

(a) Don Bradman (b) Sunil Gavaskar (c) Geoff Boycott (d) Graham Gooch

694. Agrology is the study of fertility of soils, whereas astrology, as everyone knows, is a study of the disposition of the planets, sun, and moon in so far as they affect the fortunes of men and women; however, what is agrostology?

(a) The study of grasses (b) The study of crop prospects based on a knowledge of the disposition of the planets (c) The study of agricultural economy (d) The study of agricultural sciences in their totality

695. Which is the fastest moving fish in the world?

(a) Marlin (b) Herring (c) Atlantic sailfish (d) Gangetic Hilsa

696. Although a storyteller for adults — the stories are often macabre — he writes delightful stories for children, *Charlie and the Chocolate Factory*, for instance. Who is the author?

(a) Patricia Highsmith (b) Agatha Christie (c) Roald Dahl (d) John Wyndham

697. When was Vigyan Bhavan, which was destroyed in a fire in April 1990, built?

(a) 1947 (b) 1950 (c) 1952 (d) 1957

698. Scripts are read in all kinds of ways, left to right, right to left, from up to down, and mixtures of these. What is a *boustrophedon* script?

(a) Reading from left to right (b) Reading from right to left (c) Reading from left to right and right to left alternately (d) Reading from up to down

699. Match the following celebrated kinds of cheese with the countries of their origin:

(a) Edam (b) Gruyere (c) Parmesan (d) Roquefort
1. Switzerland 2. Italy 3. Holland 4. France

700 What is the meaning of crepuscular?

(a) Having minute folds (b) Affected by gangrene (c) Like twilight (d) Faded

Quiz 36

701. Burma used to be a part of the British Indian Empire. In which year was it separated from India?
(a) 1935 (b) 1937 (c) 1945 (d) 1947

702. In which planet in our solar system are the days and nights shortest?
(a) Jupiter (b) Saturn (c) Uranus (d) Neptune

703. Cancer paralyses the mind of both the sufferer and his relatives; very few can accept it with equanimity. Here is someone, however, who has written a humorous poem about it, although basically he is not a poet. He concludes the poem with these lines:

'My final word, before I'm done,
Is "Cancer can be great fun".
Thanks to the nurses and Nye Bevan
The NHS is quite like a heaven
Provided one confronts the tumour
With a sufficient sense of humour.'

— Who wrote it?
(a) James Cameron (b) F.R. Leavis (c) Lord Keynes
(d) J.B.S. Haldane

704. Which heavyweight boxing champion holds the record of the maximum number of uninterrupted wins?
(a) Joe Louis (b) Rocky Marciano (c) Larry Holmes
(d) Jack Dempsey

705. Which judo player retired undefeated with 203 wins?
(a) Osamu Watanabe (b) Akiro Masayoshi (c) Yukio Yasuhiro (d) Yashuhiro Yamashita

706. Who was the conqueror of the Aztecs of Mexico in the sixteenth century?
(a) Diego de Velazquez (b) Hernando Cortez
(c) Montezuma (d) Charles V of Spain

707. What is the percentage of the earth covered by sea?
    (a) 75% (b) 71% (c) 68% (d) 65.5%
708. Cuba's economy is mainly dependent on
    (a) Tobacco (b) Rum (c) Corn (d) Sugar
709. Which is Europe's longest river?
    (a) Tiber (b) Volga (c) Danuba (d) Rhine
710. She was the model of fidelity. During her husband's long absence she was pursued by many suitors, but fobbed them off by various stratagems. Who was this wife of Greek mythology?
    (a) Clytemnestra (b) Medea (c) Penelope (d) Persephone
711. When is a baby called premature?
    (a) Born before the 30th week (b) Born before the 32nd week (c) Born before the 36th week (d) Born before the 37th week
712. Satyajit Ray's Apu trilogy, *The Song of the Road* (*Pather Panchali*), *The Unvanquished* (*Aparajito*), and *The World of Apu* (*Apur Sansar*) was based on two interrelated novels by a Bengali novelist. Can you name him? (Bengalis should skip this quiz, if they have a sense of decency)
    (a) Bimal Mitra (b) Rabindranath Tagore (c) Tarashankar Bandyopadhyay (d) Bibhutibhusan Bandyopadhyay
713. To make people of the world environment conscious which day of the year is observed as the World Environment Day?
    (a) 15 March (b) 5 May (c) 5 June (d) 15 September
714. Which is the country of domicile of Giant Pandas?
    (a) Russia (b) China (c) Zambia (d) Peru
715. Gabriel Garcia Marquez, author of *One Hundred Years of Solitude* and *Chronicle of a Death Foretold*, is an eminent South American novelist who was awarded the Nobel Prize in Literature in 1982. Which country does he belong to?
    (a) Mexico (b) Peru (c) Chile (d) Colombia

716. In Hindustani classical music each *gharana*, or tradition of the house, has a different style of singing. To which *gharana* did Ustad Bade Ghulam Ali Khan belong?
(a) Kirana (b) Patiala (c) Agra (d) Gwalior

717. Copernicus, the Polish astronomer, propounded the heliocentric theory of the universe (the earth revolves round the sun) around 1512. As early as the fifth century an Indian astronomer suggested precisely this. Who was he?
(a) Aryabhata (b) Varahamihira (c) Brahmagupta (d) Bhaskaracharya

718. In the Julian calendar — the Roman calendar revised by Julius Caesar — Kalends, Nones, and Ides were particular days of the month. All who have read Shakespeare's *Julius Caesar* will remember the Ides of March. Which day of the month are the Ides?
(a) Seventh (b) Tenth (c) Fifteenth (d) Fifth

719. What is a balneologist?
(a) A balloon-flying enthusiast (b) An expert on Intercontinental Ballistic Missiles (c) A specialist on the administration of mineral hot baths (d) A specialist who can analyse and cure hallucinatory experiences

720. What is the meaning of cognomen?
(a) Family name (b) Assumed name (c) Distorted name, like Chunky for Chandan (d) The real, as against assumed, meaning of a word

Quiz 37

721. Which one of the following countries is not a member of the United Nations?
(a) Vietnam (b) Turkey (c) Haiti (d) Switzerland

722. A tape recorder can be placed anywhere in a room except near a

(a) voltage stabilizer (b) switchboard (c) radio (d) magnet

723. How many identified natural satellites does Jupiter have?
(a) 7 (b) 12 (c) 16 (d) 6

724. Which of the following has the lowest specific gravity?
(a) Cork (b) Oak (c) Balsa (d) Aluminium

725. The admirers of Ian Fleming's James Bond books are many. If they have read all James Bond, how many books will they have read?
(a) 32 (b) 23 (c) 16 (d) 13

726. It is widely believed that the Roman emperor Caligula (A.D. 12-41) was insane. Anyway, he made an animal a Roman Senator, and made it attend sessions of the Senate. Which animal was it? To give the literary-minded a bonus, Jonathan Swift must have heartily approved the choice.
(a) A goat (b) A monkey (c) A horse (d) An ass

727. There are Christian Patron Saints to protect almost any class of people. Which saint protects careless people?
(a) St. Agatha (b) St. Michael the Archangel (c) St. Francis of Assissi (d) St. Anthony of Padua

728. For which fruit is Seville, in Spain, famous?
(a) Apples (b) Oranges (c) Grapes (d) Melons

729. Which country is the 'Sick Man of Europe'?
(a) Albania (b) Turkey (c) Poland (d) Czechoslovakia

730. What is the importance of the Mazarin Bible?
(a) It is the most controversial English translation of the Bible (b) It is the Puritan Bible (c) It is the first Bible printed from movable type (d) It was banned by the Pope in 1455 for its inaccuracy of text; the first such ban

731. Astigmatism, an eye defect, is caused by a defect in the curvature of the lens. It results in

(a) short-sightedness (b) near-sightedness (c) squint (d) distorted images

732. Francis Ford Coppola is a renowned American film director. Can you identify his film among the following? Coppolla directed *The Godfather*.
(a) *Satyricon* (b) *The Private Life of Henry VIII* (c) *The Rain People* (d) *On the Waterfront*

733. Who is the father, and who the mother, of a mule?
(a) An ass and a cow (b) A horse and a female ass (c) An ass and a mare (d) Two mules

734. What was the nationality of the poet, Khalil Gibran?
(a) Syrian (b) Lebanese (c) Iraqi (d) Libyan

735. With ecological awareness spreading, and with increasingly frequent warnings about despoiling forests, it would be interesting to know the total extent of afforested area in India. What percentage of India's landmass is covered by forests?
(a) 30% (b) 27% (c) 23% (d) less than 15%

736. How many republics are there in the Soviet Union?
(a) 10 (b) 13 (c) 15 (d) 17

737. What is the correct meaning of buxom?
(a) Healthily plump (b) Young and healthy (c) Full-bosomed (d) Pink-cheeked woman

738. What is xenophobia?
(a) Fear of war (b) Eagerness to get into a war (c) Fear of unknown persons (d) Hatred of foreigners

739. What does definitive mean?
(a) Official (b) Conclusive (c) Explanatory (d) Corrected

740. Where was woman suffrage, i.e., the right of the woman to vote, first introduced?
(a) USA (b) Britain (c) India (d) France

Quiz 38

741. What is the status of the Mandarin language in present-day China?

(a) It is the language of ageing bureaucrats, not favourably looked upon (b) It is confined to a certain class of literary writing (c) It is the official language of China (d) It is regarded as an obsolete language

742. In a light bulb what is the filament, which glows, made of?

(a) Aluminium (b) Tungsten (c) Silicon (d) Phosphorus

743. Mark Twain said that he was born with Halley's comet and hoped to die with it. His hope was fulfilled, and he died in 1910. How old would that make him, or in other words what is the periodicity of the appearance of the comet?

(a) 60 years (b) 70 years (c) 90 years (d) 75 years

744. How many satellites does the planet Mercury have?

(a) 2 (b) 3 (c) 5 (d) 0

745. Which monetary unit is the most common in the world?

(a) Dollar (b) Shilling (c) Franc (d) Pound

746. Who was the first foreign emperor to invade India through the Khyber Pass?

(a) Alexander the Great (b) Tamerlane (c) Muhammad of Ghazni (d) Muhammad Ghori

747. In which sport has Jack Nicklaus distinguished himself?

(a) Polo (b) Billiards (c) Snooker (d) Golf

748. Who discovered the source of the Nile?

(a) H.M. Stanley (b) David Livingstone (c) Captain Speke (d) Captain Cook

749. What is sledging in cricket?

(a) Sweeping away a low delivery as with a broom (b) A bowler deliberately trying to injure a batsman (c) Delivering a fast ball which reaches the stumps in a very low trajectory (d) Loudly abusing the opposing players continuously to make them lose their cool

750. A cataract operation is a surgery on the eye which results in
(a) the removal of the optical lens (b) the removal of an opaque or semiopaque film from the lens (c) the removal of opaque patches from the surface of the lens (d) making incisions on the lens to let light pass through it in a correct angle

751. The sale of iodized salt has been made compulsory in some places in India; Delhi, for example. What does the absence of iodine in minute quantities in our body cause?
(a) Loss of vitality (b) Loss of hair (c) Rheumatism (d) Goitre

752. The annual Edinburgh International Festival draws visitors from all over the world. What is it devoted to?
(a) The visual and the performing arts (b) Drama (c) Films (d) Music and drama

753. Among the following, who is considered to be the greatest ballerina of the century?
(a) Dame Margot Fontaine (b) Galina Ulanova (c) Isadora Duncan (d) Anna Pavlova

754. How many tentacles does an Octopus have?
(a) Six (b) Eight (c) Ten (d) Twelve

755. This lady lived to a ripe old age, but took her years humorously. She said, 'An archaeologist is the best husband any woman can have: the older she gets the more interested he is in her'. Who is she?
(a) Karen Blixen (b) Elizabeth Bowen (c) Agatha Christie (d) Dorothy Parker

756. Which is the least populated State in India?
(a) Sikkim (b) Meghalaya (c) Mizoram (d) Arunachal Pradesh

757. The full strength of the Lok Sabha is 545, and it will remain so till the year 2000. Which amendment to the Constitution fixed the number?
(a) 38th (b) 42nd (c) 44th (d) 46th

758. This piece of advice is meant for those who fall in with the majority, thinking and doing as the herd does. Who said, 'The fact an opinion has been widely held is no evidence whatsoever that it is not utterly absurd'?
(a) Winston Churchill (b) Leon Trotsky (c) George Bernard Shaw (d) Bertrand Russell

759. What is *origami* the Japanese art of?
(a) Flower decoration (b) Miniature plant culture (c) Martial art (d) Paper folding

760. What does mucilage mean?
(a) A gluey substance (b) Waste matter from the body (c) Cane juice (d) A cementing agent

Quiz 39

761. Which is the first country to have adopted a national flag?
(a) England (b) Denmark (c) Netherlands (d) France

762. When you come to think of it the invention of the safety pin was the work of a genius. Who was he?
(a) Walter Hunt (b) Sigmund Pffaf (c) George Stephenson (d) Jules Verne

763. Which is the planet nearest to the sun?
(a) Mercury (b) Jupiter (c) Mars (d) Juno

764. What is a hectometre?
(a) 10 metres (b) 100 metres (c) 10 kilometres (d) 100 kilometres

765. Written about the World War II years, *The Tin Drum* has acquired the status of a modern classic. Can you identify another book by the same author in the following list?
(a) *The Bellarosa Connection* (b) *The Flounder* (c) *The Crying of Lot 49* (d) *Slaughterhouse-5*

766. In which country is the battlefield Waterloo where Napoleon was defeated?

(a) Belgium (b) Holland (c) England (d) Denmark

767. In ancient Egyptian mythology who was the goddess of love and joy?

(a) Isis (b) Tauret (c) Hathor (d) Maat

768. Why is Assam so flood-prone?

(a) The river beds are shallow (b) Heavy rains in the catchment areas (c) Frequent release of large volumes of water by the dams (d) Frequent changes in the course of the river Brahmaputra

769. Which is the world's largest producer of coffee?

(a) Uganda (b) Brazil (c) Liberia (d) Congo

770. By what name are the modern English translations of the New Testament (1961) and the Old Testament (1970) known?

(a) The New Authorized Version (b) Modern English Bible (c) The Revised Standard Version (d) New English Bible

771. What is anorexia?

(a) A nervous disorder causing periodic forgetfulness (b) A disorder involving abnormal loss of appetite (c) Inability to read properly despite above average intelligence (d) Inability to retain food in the stomach, throwing it up

772. Collage (literally, pasting) is a technique in art consisting of cutting natural or manufactured materials and pasting them to a painted or unpainted surface. Which famous painter was the first to use it?

(a) Picasso (b) Gris (c) Braque (d) Mondrian

773. Among primates, other than man, which has the most highly developed brain?

(a) Ape (b) Lemur (c) Monkey (d) Chimpanzee

774. P.G. Wodehouse wrote about 120 books, many featuring Bertie Wooster and his inimitable 'gentleman's gentleman' Jeeves. In which book do both these characters appear for the first time?

(a) *Carry on, Jeeves* (b) *Summer Lightning* (c) *Uneasy Money* (d) *The Man with Two Left Feet*

775. The first three universities in India were founded in 1857. These were the universities of Calcutta, Bombay, and Madras. The next university was founded thirty years later, in 1887. Which was it?
   (a) Allahabad University (b) Banaras Hindu University (c) Mysore University (d) Osmania University

776. This British General was a bit of a classical scholar, and after he had conquered Sind he sent a cable to England consisting of one word: *peccavi*, meaning, 'I have sinned'. Who was this Latin punster?
   (a) Charles Metcalfe (b) Charles Napier (c) Lord Auckland (d) Charles Fraser

777. Which letter of the English alphabet is the easiest to transmit in the Morse code, requiring a very slight depression of the telegraph key?
   (a) t (b) i (c) s (d) e

778. What is psychologism?
   (a) The theory that all diseases are caused by psychological factors (b) The claim that all diseases can be cured by psychoanalysis (c) The theory that psychology is the foundation of philosophy (d) The theory that the human psyche can be read completely by applying scientific methods

779. What does ambience mean?
   (a) Background music (b) Undecisiveness (c) Atmosphere of a place (d) Difficulty

780. What is livid?
   (a) Deep red (b) Black and blue (c) Pale (d) Discoloured

Quiz 40

781. What is the normal period of office of the French President?

(a) Four years (b) Five years (c) Six years (d) Seven years

782. One planet in the night sky is easily identifiable because of its reddish hue. Which?
(a) Jupiter (b) Mars (c) Saturn (d) Mercury

783. Boris Pasternak, the Russian poet and novelist, suffered under official Soviet displeasure, so much so that he was forced to refuse the Nobel Prize. His masterpiece, *Dr. Zhivago*, could not be published in the USSR. In which country was it published in 1957?
(a) USA (b) Britain (c) France (d) Italy

784. Which country won the World Cup in football in 1990?
(a) England (b) Argentina (c) West Germany (d) Italy

785. Who was the World Heavyweight Boxing champion in 1987?
(a) Larry Holmes (b) Terry Spinks (c) Mike Tyson (d) Carl Williams

786. The ancient city of Nineveh was the capital of the Assyrian empire and became famous under such rulers as Sennacherib and Assurbanipal. The city fell in 617 B.C. In which country would it fall now?
(a) Iraq (b) Iran (c) Syria (d) Egypt

787. Which is the easternmost, westernmost and northernmost State in the United States?
(a) Montana (b) California (c) Alaska (d) Washington

788. Japan has now a very strong automobile industry and competes with the United States for the top position in the world. Which company is Japan's number 1?
(a) Nissan (b) Toyota (c) Honda (d) Isuzu

789. '... in Aleppo once,/Where a malignant and turban'd Turk/Beat a Venetian and traduc'd the State/I took by th' throat the circumcised dog/And smote him — thus' — says Othello. Where is Aleppo?

(a) Turkey (b) Jordan (c) Syria (d) Lebanon
790. With which book does the Bible end?
(a) Ephesians (b) Revelation (c) Philemon (d) Jude
791. What is the function of Vitamin K?
(a) Prevents loss of hair (b) Prevents loss of sexual power (c) Helps the functioning of the pancreas (d) Helps blood-clotting
792. Which English poet illustrated all his major work himself?
(a) Andrew Marvell (b) Percy Bysshe Shelley (c) William Blake (d) Dante Gabriel Rossetti
793. National Parks are now spread all over the country, wherever there are afforested areas. Which is India's first National Park?
(a) Sunderbans (b) Keoladeo National Park (c) Periyar National Park (d) Corbett National Park
794. For how long have cockroaches infested the earth?
(a) Since A.D. 40 (b) 10,000 years (c) 230 million years (d) 350 million years
795. Whose detective is Inspector Ghote?
(a) H.R.F. Keating (b) P.D. James (c) Dorothy L. Sayers (d) Rex Stout
796. India's 'teeming millions' number 680.5 million. What is India's ranking by population in the world?
(a) 1 (b) 2 (c) 3 (d) 4
797. The science of medicine was quite advanced in ancient India, and some doctors were contemporaries of the Roman physician, Galen. Who wrote the earliest text of Indian medicine?
(a) Charaka (b) Susruta (c) Dhanwantari (d) Agnivesh
798. Which among the following philosophers was awarded the Nobel Prize for Literature (yes, Literature)?
(a) Karl Jaspers (b) Henri Bergson (c) F.H. Bradley (d) Noam Chomsky

799. Silver for the 25th anniversary, gold for the 50th, and diamond for the 60th. Anything for the 40th?
(a) Emerald (b) Ruby (c) Turquoise (d) Pearl

800. What does exacerbate mean?
(a) To anger (b) To try one's patience (c) To worsen (d) To criticise

Quiz 41

801. *Anti-Duhring* is one of the most important documents of the Communist movement. Who among the following wrote it?
(a) Marx (b) Engels (c) Bukharin (d) Trotsky

802. Who were the first to notice that a snowflake has six sides?
(a) The Chinese (b) The Russians (c) The English (d) The Swedes

803. There are still people who are happier with the Fahrenheit scale of temperature, and the Centigrade reading has to be translated for them. How will you convert a Centigrade reading into the Fahrenheit equivalent?
(a) Add 40, multiply by 4, divide by 7 (b) Divide by 2, multiply by 5, add 32 (c) Multiply by 9, divide by 5, add 32 (d) Subtract 60, multiply by .8

804. Which rock is closest to marble?
(a) Gneiss (b) Dolomite (c) Limestone (d) Basalt

805. In whose books is Miss Marples the amateur detective?
(a) Edgar Wallace (b) P.D. James (c) Agatha Christie (d) Ellery Queen

806. Which is the first structure of Mughal architecture in India?
(a) The Qutab Minar (b) Buland Darwaza (c) Humayun's Tomb (d) Jama Masjid, Delhi

807. Which king built the Tower of London?

(a) William the Conqueror (b) Henry IV (c) Henry VIII (d) Elizabeth I

808. In which European country is the city of Strasbourg?
(a) France (b) Germany (East) (c) Germany (West) (d) Belgium

809. Which is the deepest lake in the world?
(a) Lake Victoria (b) Lake Ontario (c) Lake Michigan (d) Lake Baikal

810. One spurns the advances of an *apsara* at one's peril. Arjuna did that, when he was receiving military training in heaven; he spurned Urvashi. What curse did Urvashi utter?
(a) That Arjuna would be the killer of his teacher (b) That Arjuna would be bettered by someone else in arms training (c) Arjuna would seek the love of one woman above all, but he would have to share her with others (d) That he would become a eunuch

811. The normal human body temperature is, as we all know, 98.4 Fahrenheit. What is it on the Centigrade scale?
(a) 39.2° (b) 38.5° (c) 36.9° (d) 41.2°

812. Whales often move together in the sea. What is a group of whales called?
(a) A pack (b) A troop (c) A school (d) A cluster

813. The French architect Le Corbusier's most ambitious work was the design and construction of the city of Chandigarh. Which of the following buildings did he design?
(a) The Secretariat (b) The University complex (c) The Assembly Building (d) The High Court

814. Sarah Kemble Siddons, often referred to as Mrs. Siddons, was a great Shakespearian actress. Her performance in one of the following roles is said to be unequalled. Which?
(a) As Ophelia in *Hamlet* (b) As Cordelia in *King Lear* (c) As Calpurnia in *Julius Caesar* (d) As Lady Macbeth in *Macbeth*

815. Bees cannot distinguish one of the following colours. Which?
(a) Violet (b) Blue (c) Purple (d) Yellow

816. There is a difference between a country stocking the largest number of library books and a country having the largest library in the world, as in the former case a very large number of books may be dispersed among numerous libraries, as in the USSR. Which is the world's single largest library?
(a) The British Museum Library, London (b) Bibliotheque Nationale, Paris (c) The Library of Congress, Washington (d) New York Public Library

817. The first relics of India's ancient cities were noticed by Sir Alexander Cunningham when he found some strange unidentified seals near Harappa in Punjab. In 1922 another person found further seals at Mohenjo Daro in Sind. Who is the other person?
(a) Sir John Marshall (b) P.D. Singh (c) Hamidulla Khan (d) R.D. Banerji

818. Between two Five Year Plans of India there was once a gap of three years. Which particular Plan took a three-year-late start?
(a) Third (b) Fourth (c) Sixth (d) Eighth

819. Who discovered the North Pole on 6 April 1909?
(a) Robert Edwin Peary (b) Frederick Albert Cook
(c) Roald Amundsen (d) Umberto Nobile

820. What is the meaning of opprobrius?
(a) Expressing scorn or abuse (b) Praiseworthy
(c) Conflicting (d) Loud-mouthed

Quiz 42

821. How many times has Poland been partitioned by foreign powers and appropriated among themselves with the object of removing the country from the face of the map?
(a) Once (b) Twice (c) Three times (d) Four times

822. The absolute zero is the lowest temperature theoretically attainable, at which the particles constituting matter would be at rest. This is
(a) -80°C (b) -113°C (c) -237°C (d) -273°C

823. The magnitude and intensity of an earthquake is measured by the
(a) Fischer scale (b) Tropsch scale (c) Avery scale (d) Richter scale

824. Gasohol, as the name suggests, is a compound made to save gasoline. Gasoline is mixed with ethyl alcohol in a certain proportion to obtain the fuel-efficient compound. Can you give the correct proportion?
(a) 90% gasoline and 10% ethyl alcohol (b) 80% gasoline and 20% ethyl alcohol (c) 60% and 40% (d) 50% and 50%

825. *The Catcher in the Rye* is a novel about the innocence of adolescence which remains incorruptible, even in the predatory city of New York. It still remains a very popular novel; in fact, it is *the* novel of innocence. Who wrote it?
(a) J.D. Salinger (b) F. Scott-Fitzgerald (c) John Updike (d) Saul Bellow

826. Who was the British Prime Minister when India became independent?
(a) Winston Churchill (b) Aneurin Bevan (c) Anthony Eden (d) Clement Attlee

827. Which is the highest mountain peak in India?
(a) K2 (b) Nanga Parbat (c) Mt. Everest (d) Kanchenjanga

828. Which is the world's top oil-exporting country?
(a) Saudi Arabia (b) Nigeria (c) Iran (d) Iraq

829. Brahma begat ten sages who are known as *prajapatis*. Who, among the following, was not a *prajapati*?
(a) Angira (b) Pulastya (c) Viswamitra (d) Vashistha

830. L-dopa, or L-dihydroxyphenylalanine to give its full name, is a drug to cure

(a) Cancer (b) Impotence (c) Parkinson's disease (d) Congenital idiocy

831. Aldus Manutius (1450-1515) was a Venetian humanist scholar, who is remembered today because (a) he wrote an excellent commentary of the New Testament (b) his treatise on personal law is still studied with respect (c) his Greek-Italian dictionary was the first bilingual dictionary ever produced (d) he was an excellent typographer and designed the italic face

832. How does a tiger demarcate its domain in the forest against intrusion by other tigers?
(a) It stamps on shrubbery on the borders of its domain (b) It drops its stool at regular intervals to connect the border of its domain (c) It demarcates the border by urinating along it (d) It rubs its pelt on the trees along the border to leave its particular scent

833. *Hobson-Jobson* is the indispensable guide to Anglo-Indian English during the Raj. Who compiled it?
(a) Sir William Jones (b) E.B. Cowell and F.W. Thomas (c) Henry Yule and A.C. Burnell (d) Monier Monier-Williams

834. I see your body in the sinuous creeper, your gaze
        in the startled eyes of the deer,
    your cheek in the moon, your hair in the plumage
        of peacocks,
    and in the tiny ripples of the river I see your
        sidelong glances,
    but alas, my dearest, nowhere do I find your
        whole likeness.
— These are some lines from one of the most celebrated Sanskrit poems. Can you identify the source?
(a) Kumarasambhava (b) Ritusamhara (c) Gita Govinda (d) Meghaduta

835. In her long reign over India, around fifteen years, Indira Gandhi made a large number of amendments to the Constitution. How many were they in number?

(a) 30 (b) 32 (c) 36 (d) 39

836. How many letters of the alphabet make the Roman numbering system?

(a) 4 (b) 5 (c) 6 (d) 7

837. Penny-farthing used to be the name of a particular kind of transport. What was it?

(a) A cheap tram ride (b) A short-distance train (c) A cycle with one large wheel and another very small wheel (d) Horse-drawn buggies used as public transport

838. What does officious mean?

(a) Bureaucratic (b) Taking the rule-book too seriously (c) Unnecessarily eager to offer one's services (d) Foolishly aware of one's importance

839. Which among the following is another work by the painter of *Mona Lisa*, Leonardo da Vinci?

(a) *Madonna of the Rocks* (b) *Pieta* (c) *The Sistine Madonna* (d) *Bacchus and Ariadne*

840. Which country was the first to domesticate cats?

(a) Persia (b) Siam (c) England (d) Egypt

Quiz 43

841. Who was the first President of the United Nations General Assembly?

(a) Trygve Lie (b) Vijaylakshmi Pandit (c) U Thant (d) Krishna Menon

842. Einstein's Theory of Relativity, $E=mc^2$, was a theoretical formulation. How was it experimentally proved correct?

(a) By a solar eclipse (b) By the atom smasher (c) By a lunar eclipse (d) By a space probe

843. The poet seems to have distilled human wisdom in this couplet, when he wrote:

> I'm tired of love; I'm still more tired of rhyme
> But money gives me pleasure all the time.

— Who is he?
(a) Oscar Wilde (b) Ogden Nash (c) Lord Bowen
(d) Hillaire Belloc

844. Charles August Lindbergh's first ever solo, non-stop, transatlantic flight from New York to Paris, in his *Spirit of St. Louis*, was made in
(a) 1927 (b) 1921 (c) 1931 (d) 1936

845. A time of 2 hours 20 minutes used to be the marathon record. Who broke it?
(a) Jesse Owens (b) Archie Hahn (c) Fred Lorz
(d) Jim Peters

846. India is +5½ hours from GMT. Which place is +12 hours?
(a) New Zealand (b) Papua New Guinea (c) Cook Islands (d) Vladivostok

847. What is Calcutta's subway system called?
(a) Subway (b) Underground (c) Metro (d) Tube

848. Demographers predict that 95% of the global population growth in the next 35 years will be in the developing countries and these are not in a position at all to deal with the new arrivals. Which country will witness the most explosive growth?
(a) China (b) India (c) Bangladesh (d) Africa

849. Kinshasha is the capital city of
(a) Lesotho (b) Ghana (c) Zaire (d) Zimbabwe

850. Androcles was a Roman slave. Which animal was he friendly with?
(a) Tiger (b) Lion (c) Hunting dog (d) Cheetah

851. Which insect is the greatest disease carrier?
(a) Housefly (b) Cockroach (c) Rat (d) Mosquito

852. Of the renowned American Symphony Orchestras which is the earliest?

(a) New York Philharmonic Orchestra (b) Boston Symphony Orchestra (c) Los Angeles Philharmonic Orchestra (d) Chicago Symphony Orchestra

853. Of the following sources of noise pollution which one is capable of causing permanent damage to one's hearing?

(a) Doordarshan (b) Rock music (c) Power drill (d) Motor-cycle without a silencer

854. Which is the fastest moving snake in the world?

(a) Russell's Viper (b) King Cobra (c) Black Mamba (d) Indian Krait

855. Who wrote *The Necessity of Atheism* when he was a student and was expelled by his college for doing so?

(a) Lord Byron (b) John Stuart Mill (c) Percy Bysshe Shelley (d) Bertrand Russell

856. From Kashmir to Kanyakumari — this is how the northern and southern ends of India are commonly referred. What is the distance between the two ends?

(a) 3080 km (b) 3150 km (c) 3214 km (d) 3460 km

857. The first census after independence showed the country's literacy rate at an appalling 16.7%. We don't yet have the figures for the 1991 census, but what was the literacy rate in 1981?

(a) 29% (b) 33.6% (c) 34.4% (d) 36.2%

858. To the original five subjects on which the Nobel Prize is awarded was added a sixth subject, Economics. When was the Nobel Memorial Prize in Economic Science first awarded?

(a) 1967 (b) 1969 (c) 1971 (d) 1973

859. A4 is the international size of a certain commodity. Which?

(a) Book (b) Bra (c) Paper (d) A drawing nib

860. What is the meaning of acerbity?

(a) Clarity (b) Bitterness (c) Acuteness (d) Obstinacy

Quiz 44

861. Although one person is credited as being 'the father of the hydrogen bomb', actually two persons working together made the bomb possible. They are:
(a) John van Neumann and Edward Teller (b) Otto Hahn and Leo Szilard (c) Von Weizacker and Edward Teller (d) Wolfgang Pauli and Enrico Fermi

862. In which country do robots constitute a noticeable workforce?
(a) USA (b) Italy (c) Japan (d) Sweden

863. Trofim Denisovish Lysenko was a Soviet agronomist. However he became famous in another field, under the patronage of Stalin. After Stalin, along with many of Stalin's proteges', his theories were debunked. In which field did he attain eminence?
(a) Psychology (b) Education (c) Genetics (d) Soil Chemistry

864. What is a Mach number?
(a) It is the speed at which a machine runs with optimal efficiency (b) It is the ratio of speed between a flying object and the speed of light (c) It is the ratio of speed between a flying object and the speed of sound (d) It is the total number of neutrons and protons in nucleus of an atom

865. How many earthly years make a cosmic year?
(a) 100,000,000 years (b) 200,000,000 years (c) 250,000,000 years (d) 350,000,000 years

866. In a classic featuring an adventure by the sea, which sailor dreamed of toasted cheese?
(a) Captain Ahab (b) Captain Kidd (c) Long John Silver (d) Ben Gunn

867. India has been endowed with good seaports from the pre-Christian times and there are records of maritime trading with Ceylon, Burma, and South-East Asia. Which was the principal port in the Ganges basin in Mauryan times?

(a) Bhrigukaccha (b) Supara (c) Champa (d) Tamralipti

868. The capital of the ancient kingdom of the Cholas also has a magnificent specimen of Chola temple architecture. Where is it?
(a) Mamallapuram (b) Thanjavur (c) Kanchipuram (d) Madurai

869. What is the total number of States and political units in the continent of Africa, till 1990?
(a) 37 (b) 45 (c) 49 (d) 51

870. This country is so full of lakes that it is called 'The Land of Thousand Lakes'. Which is it?
(a) Denmark (b) Holland (c) Finland (d) Switzerland

871. The Prophet ordained that his followers should read the *namaz* so many times a day. How many?
(a) Four (b) Five (c) Six (d) Eight

872. Considerable progress has been made in the area of *in vitro* fertilization. What exactly is it?
(a) Artificial insemination (b) Donor insemination (c) Fertilization and development of the foetus outside the mother's uterus (d) Conception of a human embryo outside the mother's body

873. Among the domesticated animals the popularity of cats is quite high. Which country has the largest number of domestic cats?
(a) Egypt (b) Iran (c) Thailand (d) The United States

874. Hermitage is one of the most famous museums of art in the world, possessing more than 40,000 drawings, 500,000 engravings, and 8000 paintings of the Flemish, French, Dutch, Spanish, and the Italian schools. Where is it located?
(a) Amsterdam (b) Leningrad (c) Paris (d) Boston

875. This story is known to most godfearing editors of publishing houses; still it is so good that it bears repeating. A book was submitted to a publisher, and the editor rejected it. It went to another publisher;

here too the editor rejected it. The first editor died of a heart attack within a month, and the second committed suicide, hanging himself from a tree, wearing a bra and panties. The third editor passed it and later won the Nobel Prize for Literature. Which book was it?

(a) Samuel Beckett's *Waiting for Godot* (b) Bernard Shaw's *Mrs Warren's Profession* (c) Robert Graves's *The White Goddess* (d) T.S. Eliot's *The Waste Land*

876. The rural population, as compared to the urban, is steadily declining in India. Which State has achieved the greatest urbanization?

(a) Maharashtra (b) West Bengal (c) Kerala (d) Punjab

877. The movement for consumer protection gained a tremendous momentum in the 1960s. Which prominent activist gave it such urgency through his writings?

(a) Vance Packard (b) Alvin Toffler (c) Ralph Nader (d) Ernst Friedrich Schumacher

878. What is the sidereal month?

(a) The time needed for the moon to go through its complete cycle of phases (b) The time required by the moon to return to the same position relative to a fixed star (c) A standard 30 days (d) The month which falls short of 31 or 30 days

879. King Gordius of Phrygia had the pole of his wagon fastened to the yoke in a knot which could not be untied. An oracle said that he who could untie it would rule Asia. Who had the ready intelligence to simply cut the Gordian knot with his sword?

(a) Tamerlane (b) Hannibal (c) Alexander the Great (d) Pericles

880. What is the meaning of parsimony?

(a) Spendthrift habit (b) Greed for money (c) A silvery-white crystalline metal (d) Extreme reluctance to spend money

Quiz 45

881. Both Ambassadors and High Commissioners represent their countries; why then are some countries represented by High Commissioners?

(a) Depends on the importance of the representation (b) High Commissioners come from the Third World countries (c) Non-aligned countries are represented by High Commissioners (d) Only Commonwealth countries exchange High Commissioners

882. 'You've never had it so good', a Prime Minister told his countrymen prophetically. Which Prime Minister?

(a) Harold Macmillan (b) Harold Wilson (c) Pierre Elliott Trudeau (d) Jawaharlal Nehru

883. Of the following geological eras, in which did early man appear in Africa?

(a) Pliocene (b) Trissic (c) Jurassic (d) Pleistocene

884. Who was the first English poet to be officially given the title of Poet Laureate?

(a) Ben Jonson (b) John Donne (c) John Dryden (d) Alexander Pope

885. Which country invented backstroke swimming?

(a) Japan (b) China (c) India (d) Egypt

886. Both historical and mythical kings have been dice players, often losing heavily. What did Henry VIII stake and lose?

(a) The bells of St. Paul's Cathedral (b) The Tower of London (c) The Isle of Man (d) 100,000 guineas

887. Everybody knows that Sunil Gavaskar holds the record (10,122) of scoring the highest number of runs in Test cricket. Who is next?

(a) Gary Sobers (b) Vivian Richards (c) Geoffrey Boycott (d) Don Bradman

888. Which of the following wives of King Henry VIII was the mother of Queen Elizabeth I?

(a) Katharine of Aragon (b) Anne Boleyn (c) Jane Seymour (d) Catherine Howard

889. Which country has the most productive silver mines?

(a) Peru (b) Guatemala (c) Mexico (d) Colombia

890. In which Test ground did Sunil Gavaskar score his 10,000th Test run?

(a) Madras (b) Ahmedabad (c) Bombay (d) Bangalore

891. Of her five husbands who did Draupadi rely upon most to come to her succour and execute her wishes?

(a) Yudhisthira (b) Bhima (c) Arjuna (d) Sahadeva

892. What is the function of bile in the human body?
(a) It purifies waste matter in the body and processes them into urine (b) It dissolves fats and fat-soluble vitamins (c) It serves as an automatic alarm system for empty stomachs by eructation (d) It helps digest protein

893. Tigers live in quite a few Reserves in India, although not all of them offer a good view of the animal during one's short stay. Which Tiger Reserve is the best bet for the tourist?

(a) Ranthambhor (b) Sunderban (c) Mudumalai (d) Kanha

894. Which Indian batsman holds the record for scoring the most runs against Pakistan in a Test series?
(a) Mohinder Amarnath (b) Polly Umrigar (c) Sunil Gavaskar (d) Chetan Chauhan

895. How many caterpillars of the silk moth have to be boiled alive in order to obtain a pound of silk?
(a) 800 (b) 2000 (c) 3000 (d) 500

896. The Dadasaheb Phalke Award, the most prestigious award in the film industry, is made for signal contribution to Indian films. Who won the award in 1989?

(a) Satyajit Ray (b) Shabana Azmi (c) Lata Mangesh-kar (d) Kishore Kumar

897. Shares of established and prestigious companies are called blue chips, because
(a) the colour blue is associated with aristocracy
(b) chips of the highest value in casino gambling are blue in colour (c) at one time ownership certificates of very important companies were issued in the form of enamelled blue discs (d) at one time the share certificates used to be printed on blue parchment.

898. What is the Stanford-Binet test?
(a) A blood test to detect the AIDS virus (b) An intelligence test (c) An ophthalmoscopic test to determine any injury to the retina (d) A pregnancy test to determine the sex of the foetus

899. What is a maverick?
(a) A new entrant (b) An unorthodox person (c) A whizzkid (d) One who breaks rules

900. What does malediction mean?
(a) Evil intent (b) Illness (c) Crime (d) Curse

Quiz 46

901. Editor of *Der Stürmer*, a violently anti-semite newspaper in Nazi Germany, who was this Jew-baiter convicted at the Nuremberg trials and hanged?
(a) Martin Bormann (b) Hermann Goering (c) Adolf Eichmann (d) Julius Streicher

902. Which planet appears the brightest in the night sky?
(a) Mercury (b) Mars (c) Venus (d) Jupiter

903. Sometimes used by dentists as an anaesthetic, laughing gas is so called because it produces a sense of well-being and mirth when inhaled in small quantities. What is it really?
(a) Helium (b) Nitrous oxide (c) Hydrogen (d) Ozone

904. Which is the odd man out?
   (a) Magnesium   (b) Uranium   (c) Krypton
   (d) Chromium

905. Which cricket ground has the largest official seating capacity?
   (a) Melbourne Cricket Ground (b) Eden Gardens, Calcutta (c) Lord's, London (d) Sabina Park, Jamaica

906. Between which years was India the uninterrupted hockey champion in the Olympics?
   (a) 1928-56 (b) 1936-64 (c) 1924-52 (d) 1928-64

907. The foreign invaders to India, from Alexander the Great to Muhammad of Ghor, did not settle down in India, although some of them left their governors to administer their conquests. Who was the first invader to settle down in Delhi and found an Indian empire?
   (a) Bakhtiyar Khilji (b) Ghiyasuddin (c) Qutbuddin Aibak (d) Sultan Mahmud

908. From Beijing to Urumchi is the longest railway journey in China, and it takes four and a half days. What is the train called?
   (a) *The Restless Dragon* (b) *The Red Guard* (c) *The Iron Rooster* (d) *The Red Arrow*

909. Existentialism as an attitude has deeply influenced philosophy and literature, if not man's mind. It posits that the universe is not a determined, ordered system; that each self-aware individual understands his own existence in terms of his experience; that the self is a thinking being, and has a will which can determine its actions, and therefore each individual must assume the responsibility of making choices, however much it may cause him anxiety. Who was the first existentialist philosopher?
   (a) Karl Jaspers (b) Soren Kierkegaard (c) Martin Heidegger (d) Gabriel Marcel

910. Which is the most populous city in the world?
   (a) Shanghai (b) Mexico City (c) Tokyo (d) Calcutta

911. Four elements, according to the Greek philosophers, constituted the physical universe: earth, air, fire, and water. Each possessed any two of the following qualities: heat, cold, moisture, dryness; water, for instance, was cold and wet. What were considered to be earth's qualities?

(a) Hot and dry (b) Cold and dry (c) Hot and wet (d) Cold and wet

912. Athena, in Greek mythology, who sprung from Zeus's forehead, was the goddess of

(a) wisdom (b) beauty (c) war and peace (d) fertility

913. Who founded the Society of Jesus, whose members are known as Jesuits?

(a) St. Ignatius Loyola (b) St. Francis Xavier (c) St. Francis of Assisi (d) St. Augustine of Hippo

914. What gives the human brain its energy?

(a) Glucose (b) Phosphorus (c) Vitamin C (d) Certain kinds of protein, e.g., fish

915. What kind of phobia, or fear, is lyssophobia?

(a) Morbid fear of being killed (b) Morbid fear of crowds (c) Morbid fear of insanity (d) Morbid fear of darkness

916. Of the following instruments of an orchestra which is called the same in English, French, German, and Italian? In fact, it is the only such among all orchestral instruments.

(a) Cello (b) Trombone (c) Tuba (d) Oboe

917. What is ethology?

(a) Study of the origin and the functioning of human beings and their cultures (b) Study of the modes of ideal human behaviour (c) Study of minority groups (d) Study of animal behaviour in different environments

918. Which insect has the largest number of species in the world?

(a) Butterfly (b) Beetle (c) Flea (d) Cockroach

919. 1989 was the birth centenary of an Indian who attained great fame in the field of science or mathematics. Who is he?
(a) Sir C.V. Raman (b) Sir J.C. Bose (c) P.C. Mahalanobis (d) Srinivasa Ramanujan

920. In order to promote English education in India Lord Dalhousie took the initiative to start universities in India, and between 1857 and 1887 six universities were founded. Which among the following was the earliest?
(a) Bombay (b) Madras (c) Lahore (d) Calcutta

Quiz 47

921. Who directed the group of scientists in the Manhattan Project which succeeded in creating the atom bomb in 1945?
(a) Robert Oppenheimer (b) Albert Einstein (c) Leo Szilard (d) Enrico Fermi

922. Nuclear radiation is extremely harmful for the human body, although on one organ it has the least effect. Which?
(a) Liver (b) Scrotum (c) Heart (d) Brain

923. The Big Bang theory postulates the creation of the universe. It states
(a) that the universe was created as a result of an explosion in the sun (b) that the universe steadily expands, but occasionally there are explosions in the stars creating new heavenly bodies (c) that all the matter and energy in the universe was concentrated in a very small volume that exploded between 10 and 20 billion years, and the resulting expansion continues (d) that diverse kinds of matter and energy got together into a mass some 50 billion years ago, resulting in a tremendous explosion, and the universe as we know it was created

924. Which is the oldest satellite orbiting the earth?

(a) Skylab (b) Challenger (c) Salyut I (d) Luna

925. Officially recognized One-Day Internationals began in 1971 in Melbourne. When was the first century in this game scored?
(a) 1971 (b) 1972 (c) 1973 (d) 1974

926. When was the first World Cup Football played?
(a) 1930 (b) 1936 (c) 1928 (d) 1938

927. Mahmud of Ghazni found India such a profitable hunting ground that he came back again and again for plunder. How many times did he invade India?
(a) Seven (b) Eleven (c) Seventeen (d) Twenty-one

928. In which country are parents fined a heavy sum of money for producing a second child?
(a) Sweden (b) North Korea (c) China (d) Nicaragua

929. Which one of the following is *not* an official language of Switzerland?
(a) English (b) French (c) German (d) Italian

930. A debate is now raging in Europe and America about legitimizing euthanasia. What does the word literally mean?
(a) Good death (b) Medically administered death (c) Mercy killing (d) Painless killing of the terminally ill

931. In Greek mythology Daedalus was a very skilled craftsman. After he built the Minotaur's labyrinth in Crete, King Minos refused to let him leave the island. Daedalus then built wax wings to fly out of the island. Was he successful in his escape attempt?
(a) Yes, he escaped to Sicily (b) He took off, but the sun melted his wax wings and he fell into sea and was drowned (c) The wings were so heavy that they didn't give him any lift (d) As he was about to set off, he was apprehended by King Minos's guards

932. Who discovered Vitamins A, B and D?
(a) Linus Pauling (b) E.V. McCollum (c) D.R.S. Waksman (d) E.B. Chain

933. How much blood does the heart of an average human being pump every minute?
(a) 2.5 litres (b) 4 litres (c) 5 litres (d) 6.2 litres

934. In which chronological order do the following composers come?
(a) Bach (b) Beethoven (c) Mozart (d) Wagner

935. Ebony wood, dark in colour, gives its name to the colour of the skin of some blacks. Why is it used extensively in cabinetmaking?
(a) Black furniture with a hard polish is much valued in the houses of the wealthy (b) Ebony wood is hard and durable (c) It is soft and lends itself easily to delicate carving (d) It happens to be the only wood which is not subject to dry rot

936. There is an animal whose fingerprints are close to those of human beings. Which?
(a) Baboon (b) Gorilla (c) Orangutan (d) Chimpanzee

937. Letterpress printers used to reserve the largest space in their type case for this letter of the alphabet, because its use was most frequent. Which is it?
(a) e (b) s (c) r (d) a

938. As a result of indiscriminate hunting and denudation of the Sunderbans the tiger population declined alarmingly. When was Project Tiger launched to protect the tiger and improve its habitat?
(a) 1968 (b) 1973 (c) 1976 (d) 1977

939. It is well known that the efforts of Raja Rammohun Roy went a long way towards the abolition of the practice of widow murder, glorified as *sati*. It was the reforming zeal of Lord Bentinck which saw the passing of Regulation XVII which declared *sati* illegal. When was the Regulation passed?
(a) 4 January 1818 (b) 4 December 1829 (c) 4 July 1837 (d) 4 April 1853

940. What is the meaning of intransigence?

(a) Incompetence (b) Stubbornness (c) Remaining stationary (d) Difficulty in resolving (a problem)

Quiz 48

941. The Pale of Settlement was an area in Tsarist Russia where the Jews were allowed to settle, and in 1940, 2.7 million Jews lived there. By 1943 the Nazis had killed 2.45 million of them. Where did the largest and the most gruesome massacre take place?
(a) Babi Yar (b) Nikolaev (c) Odessa (d) Vilna

942. The concept of the zero existed; but who was the person who treated it as a number and made it the most important tool of mathematical calculation?
(a) Kanada (b) Brahmagupta (c) Aryabhata (d) Kapila

943. *The Shadow Lines*, the much (and justly) acclaimed novel by Amitav Ghosh, is his second work of fiction. His first was warmly greeted by the critics, Anita Desai writing, '... energy and spontaneity ... a vivid sense of the dramatic ... the engaging quality of the village folkstory-teller's pictorial representations ... extraordinary juxtaposition of ideas drawn from diverse fields ...' Can you name the author's first novel?
(a) *Under the Pipal Tree* (b) *The Wanderings of Alu, or Nachiketa Bose* (c) *The Circle of Reason* (d) *Fool's Paradise*

944. What does karate literally mean?
(a) To administer a chop (b) Unarmed combat (c) Open hand (d) Defence

945. Which sporting event is the long-distance *Tour de France*?
(a) Motor car racing (b) Motor cycle racing (c) French marathon (d) Cycling

946. The Potsdam Conference, held in July-August 1945, in which Churchill, Truman, and Stalin participated, took one of the following important decisions:

(a) To divide Germany into the East and the West (b) To establish four-power occupation zones for post-war Germany (c) To hold the war crimes trial in Nuremberg (d) To take effective steps to denazify Germany completely

947. Which town was subjected to an air raid for the first time in history?

(a) Belgrade (b) Izmir in Turkey (c) Guernica in Spain (d) Graz in Austria

948. In which city are there more than 20,000 windmills, the largest number in the world?

(a) Amsterdam (b) Copenhagen (c) Merida in Mexico (d) El Salvador

949. Gestalt psychology interprets phenomena as organized wholes, rather than as aggregates of distinct parts. The parts are determined by laws intrinsic to the whole rather than being randomly associated. Who, among the following, gave the Gestalt theory much of its impetus?

(a) Alfred Adler (b) Sigmund Freud (c) Max Wertheimer (d) Carl Gustav Jung

950. Ajmer is a place of pilgrimage for the Muslims, because there is a shrine of a Sufi saint. Who was the saint?

(a) Abdal Qadir Gilani (b) Khwaja Moinuddin Chisti (c) Jalaluddin Rumi (d) Fariduddin Attar

951. Which disease does the excess of uric acid cause?

(a) Diabetes (b) Incontinence (c) Gout (d) Malfunctioning of liver

952. Which folk singer is associated with the song 'Mr. Tambourine Man'?

(a) Pete Seeger (b) Joan Baez (c) Bob Dylan (d) B.B. King

953. A tiger is a fearless and fierce animal, and yet it hesitates to attack this animal which often lives in its territory. Which is it?

(a) Hyena (b) Wild buffalo (c) Antlered stag (d) Bear

954. There is one State in India where all the State-run tourist hotels are named after some bird or the other. Name which.

(a) Punjab (b) Haryana (c) Assam (d) Himachal Pradesh

955. One of the best introductions on Art, *The Story of Art,* is even prescribed as a textbook in many universities, so lucid is the exposition, and so comprehensive the coverage. Who is the author of this book?

(a) Ernst Gombrich (b) Emile Male (c) Erwin Panofsky (d) Herbert Read

956. Among the countries of the world India has the second largest population. What percentage of the world population is it?

(a) Around 31% (b) Around 23% (c) Around 14% (d) 12.5%

957. In the first census after independence, 1951, the life expectancy of an average Indian at birth was reckoned to be 32 years. This figure rose somewhat in 1981-86 owing to improved medical care and prospects of better geriatric management. To what did it rise?

(a) 72 (b) 63 (c) 56 (d) 49

958. Of the following agencies which received the Nobel Prize for Peace on three occasions?

(a) International Office for Refugees (b) Amnesty International (c) United Nations International Children's Emergency Fund (d) International Red Cross

959. How many litres go to make a gallon? Give the closest approximation?

(a) 5 (b) 4.5 (c) 6 (d) 5.5

960. What is the meaning of impute?

(a) Making someone responsible for something bad (b) To disprove some statement (c) To give credit for something to someone (d) To calculate

Quiz 49

961. There are millions of devout Muslims in China. During the Cultural Revolution how were they sought to be re-educated?
(a) During the *namaz* they were made to recite the Thoughts of Mao (b) They were made to demolish their own mosques and build party offices (c) They were put in charge of pigs (d) They were put in special camps where they were made to renounce Islam and proclaim their faith in the Path of Mao

962. Space satellites navigate the space with various objects. Which of the following requires the lowest altitude?
(a) Meteorological observation (b) Espionage (c) Communication (d) Space probe

963. What is a cat cracker?
(a) An atom smasher (b) A thief who specializes in prizing open steel safes (c) A unit in an oil refinery where mineral oils with high burning points are converted into fuels with low burning points (d) A naphtha cracking unit

964. Which was the first nuclear-powered submarine?
(a) *Triton* (b) *Nautilus* (c) *Dolphin* (d) *Neptune*

965. This modern classic did the round of publishers who thought it was too hot to handle, until Secker and Warburg decided to take the plunge. That was in 1944. The book is still doing very well, thank you. Which among the following is it?
(a) *Lolita* by Vladimir Nabokov (b) *Darkness at Noon* by Arthur Koestler (c) *Animal Farm* by George Orwell (d) *Lady Chatterley's Lover* by D.H. Lawrence

966. Scholarly study of Indian archaeology began in the first half of the nineteenth century. Who is called the father of Indian archaeology?
(a) James Princep (b) Alexander Cunningham (c) John Marshall (d) Sir William Jones

967. Who introduced potatoes into England?
(a) Sir Walter Raleigh (b) Sir Francis Drake (c) Captain Cook (d) Sir Philip Sidney

968. Of which country is SABENA the international airline?
(a) Norway (b) Belgium (c) Denmark (d) Netherlands

969. Which is the largest port in Germany (united)?
(a) Hamburg (b) Kiel (c) Bremerhaven (d) Wilhelmshaven

970. Vishnu had three wives. Which among the following is an outsider?
(a) Ganga (b) Yamuna (c) Lakshmi (d) Sarasvati

971. Dyslexia is a learning handicap which may affect a person of above average intelligence. Formerly dyslectic persons were considered dull-witted, although now that the chief symptom has been identified treatment is possible. What is the chief symptom?
(a) Inability to remember names (b) Lack of mathematical skill (c) Lack of capacity to think logically and consecutively (d) A disability of vision, causing a reversal of letters or words in reading and writing

972. Which is the fastest train in the world?
(a) TGV (b) Bullet (c) Intercity (d) Mallard

973. Alabaster is a favourite medium of sculptors and stonecasters, because it is
(a) the purest white (b) long-lasting and stainproof
(c) figurines made of this mineral fetch a high price
(d) soft, and therefore easily sculpted

974. *The Silent Spring* (1962) was an early and influential study on the dangers of insecticides and the consequent ecological damage. Who was the author of this book?
(a) Alvin Toffler (b) Linus Pauling (c) Rachel Carson
(d) Germaine Greer

975. Take a pair of mating rats in the full flush of adulthood and give them three years. How many will their family number, children, grandchildren, and so on, at the end of the third year?
(a) 110,000,000 (b) 220,000,000 (c) 330,000,000 (d) 440,000,000

976. *The Ginger Man*, one of the greatest comic novels written in the last fifty years, is about the adventures of Alec Sebastian Dangerfield, a law student in Dublin. Who is its author?
(a) Sean O'Connery (b) Miles O'Flaherty (c) J.P. Donleavy (d) Sean O'Faolin

977. This school in India, for the last ten years in the *Guinness Book of World Records* as the largest in the world, has 12,000 students, 400 teachers, and 600 other employees. Which is it?
(a) St. John's School, Meerut (b) Cathedral High School, Bombay (c) Yadavindra Public School, Patiala (d) South Point School, Calcutta

978. Robert Strange McNamara, who became U.S. Defense (that's how it is spelt in the USA) Secretary and President of the World Bank, came from an automobile company, where he was President. Which?
(a) Ford Motor Co. (b) Chrysler Corp. (c) General Motors (d) Cadillac Corp.

979. What is turpitude?
(a) Laziness (b) Depravity (c) Correct behaviour (d) Straightforwardness

980. What is the meaning of blasé?
(a) Bored (b) Self-satisfied (c) Overconfident (d) Cheerful

Quiz 50

981. It is their frequency of occurrence in a sentence which gives structural words their importance, and

that is why in language teaching mastery over their use is greatly stressed. Which is the most frequently used word in the English language?

(a) a (b) and (c) the (d) to

982. The Montgolfiers, Joseph and Jacques, French brothers, were the first to send up a hot-air-filled balloon, as they were also the first in manned balloon flight, when their balloon sailed over Paris. In which historic year did both these events occur?

(a) 1783 (b) 1790 (c) 1793 (d) 1803

983. How much could Doordarshan have earned from advertisers for the entire *Mahabharat* series?

(a) Rs. 50 crores (b) Rs. 65 crores (c) Rs. 77 crores (d) Rs. 80 crores

984. In the pre-metricated days Englishmen sometimes tipped a tanner to the porter or suchlike. How much was it?

(a) 10s (b) 6d (c) 10d (d) 2s

985. What does contrite mean?

(a) Satisfied (b) Completed within a time-frame (c) Repentant (d) Opposite

986. In which country did the sauna — hot steam bath, basically — originate?

(a) Norway (b) Sweden (c) Finland (d) China

987. What is common between the following: Micmac, Tillamook, Kitamet, and Nitinet?

(a) They are all rivers (b) They are all names of restaurants in Nigeria (c) They are all North American Indian languages (d) They are names of successive generations of computers

988. His mother's maiden name is quite easy to remember, as it is that of a famous perfume. Of course, it is assumed that you do know some perfumes. Name the person.

(a) John Arden (b) Harold Wilson (c) Francois Mitterrand (d) William Shakespeare

989. Prudish Victorian England called a certain garment 'unmentionables'. What were they?
(a) Women's stays (b) Men's underwear (c) Trousers (d) Knickers

990. If the development of Old English had not been radically altered by the Norman Conquest, the inhabitants of England would have spoken today a language very close to
(a) High German (b) Dutch (c) French (d) Spanish

991. Guernica is a town in northern Spain which was completely destroyed by German bombers coming to the aid of the rebel Franco. The destruction of the town is the subject matter of a painting by a great painter. Can you name him?
(a) Graham Sutherland (b) Georges Braque (c) Pablo Picasso (d) Jackson Pollock

992. On the *Baisakhi* day, 13 April 1919, there was a large gathering of unarmed people at Jallianwalla Bagh in Amritsar, upon whom General Dyer's troops fired killing, even according to government estimates, 379 and injuring 1200. How many rounds were fired?
(a) 1600 (b) 1800 (c) 2000 (d) 2100

993. A lecturer in mathematics of Christ Church College, Oxford, took the three daughters of his Dean (i.e., Principal) for a boat trip in the river. Out of that grew the perennial classic, *Alice's Adventures in the Wonderland*. Who are the three daughters?
(a) Alice, Edith, and Lorina (b) Alice, Martha and Selina (c) Alice, Helena, and Martha (d) Alice, Beatrice, and Eunice

994. Maria Montessori devised a system of pre-school education which holds that a child learns naturally if placed in an environment which provides learning games suited to the child's ability and interest. What was the nationality of Maria Montessori?
(a) Italian (b) Swiss (c) French (d) American

995. A few years after the hydrogen bomb was test-detonated, the Campaign for Nuclear Disarmament, or the CND, was started, and the intellectuals lent it strong support. Which year saw the beginning of the campaign?

(a) 1952 (b) 1955 (c) 1958 (d) 1960

996. Most of the world's opium, from which heroin is ultimately derived, is grown in a region known as the Golden Triangle. Which countries form this triangle?

(a) Thailand, Burma, and Laos (b) Kampuchea, Thailand, and Burma (c) Vietnam, Kampuchea, and Laos (d) Malaysia, Thailand, and Kampuchea

997. What was the basic step in the development of skyscrapers?

(a) The invention of fire-safety devices (b) The perfection of concrete piles (c) The invention of the pneumatic drill (d) The invention of the safety elevator

998. What is a dedicated computer?

(a) It performs the particular kind of task assigned to it (b) It makes no mistakes whatsoever in its function (c) It will function only for one operator who has been handling it from the beginning (d) It simply means a computer dedicated by a VIP to the nation or some such noble thing

999. When did the Parsees, followers of Zoroastrianism, first emigrate to India?

(a) Fourteenth century (b) Eleventh century (c) Ninth century (d) Eighth century

1000. What is the meaning of inveigle?

(a) To abuse (b) To persuade (c) To preach (d) To lead astray

Answers

1. (d)
2. (a)
3. (a)
4. (d)
5. (c)
6. (c)
7. (b)
8. (d)
9. (b)
10. (a)
11. (b)
12. (c)
13. (d), (b), (c), (a)
14. (c)
15. (b)
16. (c)
17. (c)
18. (d)
19. (c)
20. (d)
21. (d)
22. (c)   The Bengal
         Chemical and
         Pharmaceutical
         Works
23. (d)
24. (a)
25. (b)
26. (a)
27. (a)
28. (c)
29. (b)
30. (c)
31. (c)
32. (b) and (c)
33. (c)
34. (b)

35. (d)
36. (a)
37. (a)
38. (c)
39. (c)
40. (d)
41. (b)
42. (d)
43. (b)
44. (a)
45. (c)
46. (c)
47. (c)
48. (c)
49. (c)
50. (d)
51. (d)
52. (a)
53. (d)
54. (d)
55. (d)
56. (c)
57. (d)
58. (c)
59. (d)
60. (c)
61. (d)
62. (c), (b), (d), (a)
63. (a)
64. (b)   developed from
         (d)
65. (b)
66. (b)
67. (b)   in Urengoi
68. (c)
69. (a)
70. (c)
71. (b)

72. (c)	110. (a)
73. (a)	111. (b)
74. (c)	112. (d)
75. (d)	113. (d)
76. (d)	114. (b)
77. (d)	115. (d)
78. (a)	116. (b)
79. (d)	117. (a)
80. (b)	118. (d)
81. (a) in 1954, to developments in S-E Asia	119. (c)
	120. (d)
	121. (d)
82. (b)	122. (d)
83. (d)	123. (c)
84. (a) or (b)	124. (c)
85. (d)	125. (c)
86. (c)	126. (c)
87. (c)	127. (d)
88. (a)	128. (c)
89. (c) and (d)	129. (c)
90. (d)	130. (d) Now called Sarnath
91. (c)	
92. (c)	131. (c)
93. (b)	132. (d)
94. (a)	133. (c)
95. (d)	134. (c)
96. (b)	135. (d)
97. (d)	136. (b)
98. (d)	137. (a)
99. (c)	138. (c)
100. (c)	139. (a)
101. (c)	140. (a)
102. (b) 248 years	141. (c)
103. (b)	142. (b) 88 days
104. (b)	143. (a)
105. (b)	144. (a) 20 years 145 days
106. (c)	
107. (b)	145. (c)
108. (a)	146. (c) 64 years
109. (c)	147. (a)

148. (b)
149. (c)
150. (c)
151. (b)
152. (a)
153. (c)
154. (d)   50" long; wing
            span 9'–10"
155. (a)
156. (c)
157. (c)   1784
158. (d)   Means Commis-
            sioner
159. (a)
160. (c)
161. (a)
162. (b)
163. (b)
164. (c)
165. (a)
166. (a)
167. (a)   18,352 km
168. (b)
169. (c)   Jean Buridan
            (1295-1356),
            French
            philosopher
170. (d)
171. (c)
172. (d)
173. (b)
174. (d)
175. (c)
176. (d)
177. (c)
178. (d)
179. (d)
180. (a)

181. (b)   The first
            emperor of
            China
182. (c)
183. (b)
184. (c)
185. (c)
186. (b)
187. (a)
188. (a)
189. (a)   in Rome
190. (c)
191. (d)
192. (c)   1748; Bolshoi
            1773
193. (b)
194. (c)
195. (d)
196. (a)
197. (d)
198. (d)
199. (b)
200. (c)
201. (c)
202. (d)
203. (d)
204. (c)
205. (b)
206. (b)
207. (c)
208. (d)
209. (d)   His other name
            was Dharma
210. (a)
211. (c)
212. (a)
213. (c)
214. (c), (b), (a), (d)
215. (b)
216. (c)

217. (a)		256. (b)	In Madras, 1937
218. (d)		257. (c)	
219. (b)		258. (d)	
220. (b)		259. (a)	
221. (a)		260. (d)	
222. (d)		261. (b)	
223. (a)		262. (c)	
224. (a)		263. (c)	
225. (d)		264. (b)	74 times
226. (a)		265. (d)	
227. (b)		266. (b)	
228. (d)	pop. 10,073,000	267. (c)	
229. (c)		268. (d)	
230. (b)		269. (d)	
231. (b)		270. (a)	
232. (d)		271. (a)	
233. (c)		272. (b)	
234. (d)	1858; the others 1842	273. (c)	
		274. (d)	
235. (c)	1922	275. (c)	*The Lord of the Flies*
236. (a)			
237. (b)		276. (d)	
238. (d)		277. (c)	
239. (d)		278. (d)	
240. (d)		279. (d)	
241. (c)		280. (c)	
242. (b)		281. (c)	
243. (b)		282. (a)	Period of rotation 243 days
244. (d)			
245. (b)		283. (a)	
246. (b)		284. (a)	
247. (d)		285. (c)	
248. (d)		286. (d)	
249. (b)		287. (c)	
250. (a)		288. (a)	
251. (a)		289. (a)	
252. (d)		290. (b)	
253. (d)		291. (d)	
254. (b)		292. (a)	
255. (b)	1844	293. (b)	

294. (b)
295. (a)
296. (c)
297. (c)
298. (c)
299. (c)
300. (b)
301. (d)
302. (a)
303. (b)
304. (d)
305. (d)
306. (d)
307. (a)
308. (c)
309. (c)
310. (d)
311. (a)
312. (b)
313. (c)
314. (a), (d), (c), (b)
315. (d)
316. (a)
317. (c)
318. (d)
319. (c)
320. (b)
321. (b)
322. (c)
323. (c)
324. (a)
325. (c)
326. (b)   1875
327. (b)
328. (a)   10,800m
329. (d)
330. (c)
331. (b)
332. (c)
333. (a)

334. (d)
335. (c)
336. (c)
337. (a)
338. (b)
339. (a)
340. (c)
341. (b)   Her name was
            Erika Mann
342. (b)
343. (d)
344. (a)
345. (b)
346. (b)   Christ's disciple;
            came soon after
            Christ's   cruci-
            fixion, died in
            Mylapore,
            Madras
347. (a)
348. (a), (b), (c)
349. (d)
350. (c)
351. (a)
352. (c)
353. (d)
354. (d)
355. (a)
356. (b)
357. (d)
358. (a)
359. (d)
360. (b)
361. (b)
362. (a)
363. (b)
364. (c)
365. (c)
366. (d)
367. (c)

368. (c)
369. (a)
370. (a)
371. (d)
372. (b)
373. (d)
374. (b) 640 days
375. (d)
376. (d)
377. (c)
378. (d)
379. (b)
380. (d)
381. (b)
382. (b) 80+ km
383. (c)
384. (d)
385. (b)
386. (d)
387. (c)
388. (b)
389. (a)
390. (b)
391. (a)
392. (a)
393. (d)
394. (c)
395. (d)
396. (a)
397. (a)
398. (b) They are in Cambridge too, but Magdalene has a final e
399. (b)
400. (b)
401. (c)
402. (c)
403. (b)
404. (d)

405. (c)
406. (d)
407. (c) 979 m
408. (b)
409. (b)
410. (b)
411. (c)
412. (a)
413. (a)
414. (a)
415. (d)
416. (a)
417. (a)
418. (a)
419. (c)
420. (d)
421. (a) Possibly 1.5 million, or more
422. (c)
423. (c)
424. (c)
425. (c)
426. (b)
427. (c)
428. (d)
429. (c)
430. (b)
431. (c)
432. (c)
433. (a)
434. (b)
435. (b)
436. (b)
437. (d)
438. (c)
439. (c)
440. (d)
441. (b)
442. (a)
443. (b)

138

444. (c)
445. (c) Mat chairman, Referee, Judge
446. (c)
447. (c)
448. (b)
449. (c)
450. (d)
451. (d)
452. (d)
453. (d) Dharavi
454. (c)
455. (c)
456. (b)
457. (c)
458. (c)
459. (a)
460. (d)
461. (d) In 'On Going Too Far', 1927
462. (a)
463. (d)
464. (a)
465. (c)
466. (b) 1530-84, Ruler of Russia
467. (a)
468. (c)
469. (a)
470. (c)
471. (d)
472. (b)
473. (a)
474. (b)
475. (b)
476. (b) and (c)
477. (a) 1872
478. (b)
479. (b)
480. (b)
481. (c)
482. (c) 1956 at Calder Hall
483. (a)
484. (c) 1801
485. (c)
486. (b)
487. (b)
488. (d)
489. (b)
490. (b)
491. (d)
492. (d)
493. (d)
494. (a)
495. (a)
496. (c)
497. (c)
498. (c) *Treasure Island*, R.L. Stevenson
499. (d)
500. (b)
501. (a)
502. (a)
503. (b)
504. (a)
505. (b)
506. (b)
507. (d)
508. (c)
509. (c)
510. (a)
511. (d)
512. (b)
513. (c)
514. (b)
515. (b)
516. (b)
517. (b)
518. (a)

519. (d)
520. (b)
521. (c)
522. (c)
523. (b)
524. (d)
525. (c)
526. (d)
527. (b)
528. (d) Idaho, Indiana, Kansas, Kentucky, Mississippi, Ohio, Pennsylvania, Tennessee, Vermont, Michigan
529. (b)
530. (c) Shantiparva
531. (c)
532. (d)
533. (d)
534. (d)
535. (b)
536. (a)
537. (c)
538. (c) 1386
539. (d)
540. (c)
541. (c) 6.2%
542. (c)
543. (d)
544. (b)
545. (c)
546. (c)
547. (a)
548. (a)
549. (c)
550. (d)
551. (c)
552. (d)

553. (b)
554. (d)
555. (a)
556. (b)
557. (c)
558. (c)
559. (c)
560. (b)
561. (b)
562. (d)
563. (b)
564. (c)
565. (b)
566. (c)
567. (a)
568. (d)
569. (b)
570. (c)
571. (a)
572. (a)
573. (b)
574. (a)
575. (c)
576. (c)
577. (c)
578. (d)
579. (b)
580. (a)
581. (c)
582. (b)
583. (c)
584. (d)
585. (a)
586. (a)
587. (d)
588. (b)
589. (a)
590. (c)
591. (a)
592. (b)

593. (d)
594. (b)
595. (a)
596. (c)
597. (a)
598. (c)
599. (c)
600. (d)
601. (c)
602. (b)
603. (b), (d)
604. (a)
605. (d)
606. (d)
607. (d)
608. (c)   In Russia,
            7495m
609. (b)
610. (a)
611. (c)
612. (b)
613. (a)
614. (a)
615. (a)
616. (d)
617. (b)
618. (c)
619. (d)
620. (c)
621. (a)
622. (b)
623. (c)
624. (a)
625. (a)
626. (d)
627. (b)
628. (b)
629. (c)
630. (d)
631. (b)

632. (c)
633. (d)
634. (c)
635. (d)
636. (not d; the others
        are the same person)
637. (a)
638. (c)
639. (c)
640. (d)
641. (a)
642. (b)
643. (d)
644. (c)
645. (a)   At Poona
646. (a)
647. (a)
648. (c)
649. (a)
650. (b)
651. (c)
652. (a)
653. (b)
654. (a)
655. (a)
656. (a)   Fifth century
657. (b)
658. (b)
659. (c)
660. (d)
661. (d)
662. (b)
663. (b)
664. (c)
665. (b)
666. (d)
667. (c)
668. (c)
669. (d)
670. (b)

671. (d)		708. (d)
672. (c)		709. (b)
673. (d)		710. (c)	Odysseus's wife
674. (c)		711. (d)
675. (c)		712. (d)
676. (c)		713. (c)
677. (a)		714. (b)
678. (c)		715. (d)
679. (d)		716. (b)
680. (d)		717. (a)
681. (c)		718. (c)
682. (c)		719. (c)
683. (c)		720. (a)
684. (c)		721. (d)
685. (b)		722. (d)
686. (b)		723. (c)	4 large, 12 small
687. (d)		724. (a)
688. (a)	346 km	725. (d)
689. (c)		726. (c)
690. (b)		727. (d)
691. (c)		728. (b)
692. (c)		729. (b)
693. (d)	333 against India, 1990	730. (c)	Also known as the Gutenberg Bible
694. (a)	
695. (c)		731. (d)
696. (c)		732. (c)
697. (b)		733. (c)
698. (c)		734. (b)
699. (a3, b1, c2, d4)		735. (c)
700. (c)		736. (c)
701. (b)		737. (c)
702. (a)	and (b); their period of rotation is 10 hours	738. (d)
		739. (b)
		740. (a)	1920; in Britain only in 1928
703. (d)	
704. (b)		741. (c)
705. (d)		742. (b)
706. (b)		743. (d)
707. (b)		744. (d)

745. (a) More than 23 countries

746. (a)
747. (d)
748. (c)
749. (d)
750. (a)
751. (d)
752. (d)
753. (d)
754. (b)
755. (c)
756. (a)
757. (b)
758. (d)
759. (d)
760. (a)
761. (b) A.D. 1219
762. (a)
763. (a)
764. (b)
765. (b) Gunter Grass
766. (a)
767. (c)
768. (d)
769. (b)
770. (d)
771. (b)
772. (a) 1912; he pasted a commercially printed oilcloth to his cubist painting *Still Life with Chair Caning*
773. (d)
774. (d)
775. (a)
776. (b)
777. (d) A dot

778. (c)
779. (c)
780. (b)
781. (d)
782. (b)
783. (d)
784. (c)
785. (c)
786. (a)
787. (c)
788. (b)
789. (c)
790. (b)
791. (d)
792. (c)
793. (d)
794. (d)
795. (a)
796. (b)
797. (d)
798. (b)
799. (b)
800. (c)
801. (b)
802. (a)
803. (c)
804. (b)
805. (c)
806. (c)
807. (a)
808. (a)
809. (d)
810. (d)
811. (c)
812. (c)
813. (a), (c), (d)
814. (d)
815. (d)
816. (c)
817. (d)

818. (b)		858. (b)	
819. (a)		859. (c)	
820. (a)		860. (b)	
821. (c)	1772, 1793, 1795	861. (a)	
822. (d)		862. (c)	
823. (d)		863. (c)	
824. (a)		864. (c)	
825. (a)		865. (c)	
826. (d)		866. (d)	in *Treasure Island*
827. (d)		867. (d)	
828. (a)		868. (b)	
829. (c)		869. (c)	
830. (c)		870. (c)	
831. (d)		871. (b)	
832. (c)		872. (d)	
833. (c)		873. (d)	
834. (d)		874. (b)	
835. (b)		875. (c)	T.S. Eliot of
836. (d)	IVXLCDM		Faber accepted
837. (c)			it
838. (c)		876. (a)	
839. (a)		877. (c)	
840. (d)		878. (b)	
841. (b)		879. (c)	
842. (a)		880. (d)	
843. (d)		881. (d)	
844. (a)		882. (a)	
845. (d)		883. (a)	
846. (a)		884. (c)	
847. (c)		885. (d)	
848. (d)		886. (a)	
849. (c)		887. (c)	8114 runs
850. (b)		888. (b)	
851. (a)		889. (c)	
852. (a)		890. (b)	1986-87
853. (b)		891. (b)	
854. (c)		892. (b)	
855. (c)		893. (d)	
856. (c)		894. (c)	529, 1979-80
857. (d)		895. (c)	

896. (c)
897. (b)
898. (b)
899. (b)
900. (d)
901. (d)
902. (c)
903. (b)
904. (c)   The others are
            metals while it's
            a gas.
905. (a)   1,30,000
906. (a)
907. (c)
908. (c)
909. (b)
910. (b)
911. (b)
912. (c)
913. (a)
914. (a)
915. (c)
916. (c)
917. (d)
918. (b)
919. (d)
920. (d)
921. (a)
922. (d)
923. (c)
924. (d)   This Luna simp-
            ly means the
            moon
925. (b)   By Denis Amiss
            of England
926. (a)
927. (c)
928. (c)
929. (a)
930. (a)

931. (a)
932. (b)
933. (d)
934. (a), (c), (b), (d)
935. (b)
936. (c)
937. (a)
938. (b)
939. (b)
940. (b)
941. (a)
942. (b)
943. (c)
944. (c)
945. (d)
946. (b)
947. (c)
948. (c)
949. (c)
950. (b)
951. (c)
952. (c)
953. (b)
954. (b)
955. (a)
956. (c)
957. (c)
958. (d)
959. (b)
960. (a)
961. (c)
962. (b)
963. (c)
964. (a)   USA, 1960
965. (c)
966. (b)
967. (a)
968. (b)
969. (a)
970. (b)

971. (d)	986. (c)
972. (b)	987. (c)
973. (d)	988. (d) Elizabeth Arden
974. (c)	989. (c)
975. (c)	990. (b)
976. (c)	991. (c)
977. (d)	992. (a)
978. (a)	993. (a)
979. (b)	994. (a)
980. (a)	995. (c)
981. (c)	996. (a)
982. (a)	997. (d)
983. (a)	998. (a)
984. (b)	999. (d)
985. (c)	1000 (d)

GENERAL QUIZ

Here is a quizbook which spreads its net very wide, to test whethe
you are generally aware about things happening around you. You
may be a specialist, or you may have a broad interest in a subject
area or two; you are nevertheless expected to be conversant, as
citizen of the world, with all aspects of human endeavour, in all th
is around you, and in all that is happening. History, geography,
ecology, world affairs, politics, science, philosophy and religion,
medicine, sports, flora and fauna, literature and the other arts, an
above all, the Indian reality – all directly concern you. It's time you
found out how much you know and how much you need to know.

The multiple-choice format of this Rupa quizbook will make your
quest for knowledge more interesting, for the four possible
answers are relevant and are expected to lead you to discoveries
of your own.
Test your general, contemporary knowledge with *General Quiz*.

ISBN 978-81-716-7037-6
₹95

RUPA

www.rupapublications.com

www.ingramcontent.com/pod-product-compliance
Lightning Source LLC
Chambersburg PA
CBHW072207060526
44654CB00047B/1466